DATE DUE

STOTAN!

Chris Crutcher

STOTAN!

Greenwillow Books, New York

Copyright © 1986 Chris Crutcher
All rights reserved. No part of this book may be reproduced or utilized in any form
or by any means, electronic or mechanical, including photocopying, recording, or
by any information storage and retrieval system, without permission in writing from
the Publisher, Greenwillow Books, a division of William Morrow & Company,
Inc., 1350 Avenue of the Americas, New York, NY 10019.
Printed in the United States of America
First Edition   10 9 8 7 6 5 4 3 2

Library of Congress Cataloging in Publication Data
Crutcher, Chris. Stotan!
Summary: A high school coach invites members of his swimming
team to a memorable week of rigorous training that tests
their moral fiber as well as their physical stamina.
[1. Swimming—Training—Fiction. 2. High school—
Fiction. 3. Schools—Fiction] I. Title.
PZ7.C89St 1986 [Fic] 85-12712
ISBN 0-688-05715-2

IN MEMORY OF MY DAD
1922–1985
A STOTAN ALL THE WAY

STOTAN!

CHAPTER 1

November 5

We saw the notice about Stotan Week on the bulletin board just off the deep end of the pool after our early-morning workout today. It was already curling at the edges from the high humidity and chlorine content of the air, a lot the way my skin feels after a good three-hour workout.

"What's a Stotan Week?" Nortie asked, glancing quickly around at the rest of us. It sounded like a riddle.

No response; we just looked at him, then back to the notice, which read:

STOTAN WEEK

Dec. 17 to Dec. 21
8 a.m. to Noon Daily
Volunteers Only

Looking for a few good men
SEE MAX

"December 17," Nortie said. "That's the start of vacation. How come it's at the start of vacation? What's a Stotan Week?"

Jeff looked at him again. "All in favor of Nortie checking out Stotan Week with Max and reporting back to us, say 'aye.'"

Lion and I said, "Aye."

"Sorry, guys, not me. I'm not asking. I don't even want to know. You do it, Walker; you're the captain."

Max makes Nortie nervous because he's quiet and it's hard to tell what he's thinking a lot of the time. Nortie's not emotionally equipped to talk to Max.

"Nortie," I said, "I'm worried about you. You're a senior in high school. You could actually graduate if the folks in the office forget how to count. You have to learn to talk to people."

"I talk," he said, "but this is a job for the captain. This looks like one of Max's tricks. If I ask him, he'll just look at me like I'm in advanced Special Ed or try to get me to believe something really strange."

We heard the door slam and the flapping of Max's rubber thongs as he came through the equipment room toward the pool deck where we stood. Nortie nodded toward me. Max stopped in the doorway.

I said, "Hi, Max. How's it going?" I let Nortie off the hook. "What's a Stotan Week?"

Max smiled. "Take a chance; show up on the seventeenth and find out."

"Says here it's voluntary," I said. "I like to know what I'm volunteering for."

"Sometimes it's better not to know."

Nortie flinched a little. "I'll bet it's tough, huh?"

Max shrugged. "Wouldn't be surprised."

Lion walked over and sat on the low board, rocking back

and forth on his big arms, looking at Max, who's about half his size. "What happens if we decide not to volunteer?"

"You won't get the benefit of Stotan Week," Max said, and walked over to drop the thermometer in the water. He tied the long string to the ladder and let it dangle, then got the chemical testing kit out of the pump room to check the PH and chlorine levels. We had learned all we were going to learn about Stotan Week for today.

"See you guys at workout," he said.

I don't know that any of us will ever know what makes Max tick. He started coaching here at Frost my freshman year and I don't know him much better than I did the first day I walked into the pool area. Not really. He's one of those guys you only know by what they *do*. You have to guess how they *are*.

Max is Korean; his last name is Il Song. Not Korea Korean, though; Great Falls, Montana, Korean. He grew up on a ranch just outside of Great Falls—sort of a Korean cowboy, I guess—but he's also spent some time in the Orient, in Korea itself and in Japan, and his parents are from Seoul, so he has a pretty mixed background.

I'll say one thing about him straightaway: he's a tough hombre. He has a third-degree black belt in Tai Kwan Do, which is a kind of karate, and I've seen him kick an apple off the head of a guy 6'8". It doesn't matter that Lion's twice his size.

I know we'll all show for Stotan Week, whatever it is—even though it'll certainly alter the extra week of Christmas vacation we're getting this year—and I know something else: it won't be easy.

We start the early-morning workout at 5:30. Max doesn't show up for it, just leaves instructions on the board. He's always been real clear that we get out of swimming just what we put into it, and if we let down because he's not around, we'll never be that good anyway. We've been together long enough that we push each other hard without him, and the morning workouts are just conditioning, not technique, so we don't miss him as long as he lets us know what we're supposed to do. Besides, he says he hates to get up that early, but doesn't mind a bit if we do. It all works out.

The four of us have spent all our high-school years at Frost, and have been pretty much the core of the swimming team. And, except for girlfriends, have been at the core of each other's lives. Back in grade school and Junior High we swam on the summer AAU team together, so we go back a long ways. There's another member of our little group of musketeers, but she's a girl and isn't on the team, though she works out with us. That's Elaine. Talent-wise, she's probably better than any of us, except maybe Nortie, but she's out of the competition business these days—burned out at seventeen—and works out only to keep in shape and be part of our group. She's into more cosmic things now.

This should be the year I make it at least to the consolation finals at State; I'm dedicating the time between now and March to that. These past two years my times have been dropping like a rock, probably because I've worked out summers with Max instead of with the AAU team and because he has me on a monster weight program that's turning me into a big, fast, sleek piece of work. Max says when he was a kid and they wanted their ski boat to go faster, they put a bigger motor on it. It's working for me, and I plan to do some big-league butt-kicking before this year is over. Being a late developer, I have a few scores to settle.

Nortie will go again. He's gone every year—and won at

least one event each time. He's more excited this year, though, because it's his last year and because we have a chance to take a relay team, which would mean Jeff and Lion would be there too. Nortie and I both went last year, though I didn't place, and this year the school has said that if we qualify the relay, they'll pull out all the stops and send us in style.

This is the last year of swimming at Frost, which is probably why there are only the four of us on the team. None of the other schools in Spokane has a team—or a pool, for that matter—and we have to travel a long way to find meets; mostly to college towns in southeastern Washington and northern Idaho and, once a year, to Montana. Basically, that means we cost a lot more than we're worth. Plus, we never actually win a meet. We win most of the events we swim, but there aren't enough of us to take the whole thing. For one thing, we have no diver, so we lose those points, and if we swim one relay, that means we can't swim the other, so the best we can do on those is break even. Then, we have no one to take second- or third-place points in the events we do win, so we don't get much ahead. In Tri-Cities they let us swim as many events apiece as we want, to keep the meet interesting. We win that one, but then have to forfeit, legally, because we broke the rules to do it. So we may very well be the best team in the state, of any kind, that winds up each season with a row of goose eggs in the win column. We think that's pretty funny. Lion even had a bunch of T-shirts made up with our win-loss record across the chest.

The biggest problem with the early-morning workout is there's an hour between the time we finish and the time school starts, so we're just hanging out with not much to do. We can't get into the main building, and even if we could, all they have in there is books, which is not real exciting at 7:00 in the morning. What we do is head over to Dolly's Café to chow down on some of Dolly's home cooking and replenish all the vitamins and minerals we left in the pool. I choose to replenish them with what I have concluded through an independent and scientifically unsupported survey is nature's perfect breakfast: pancakes, swimming—and I mean *swimming*—in maple syrup. I see it as my job to carry on the never ending battle against tofu and bean sprouts and brown rice and other communist-inspired dishes that have obviously been smuggled into this country to show my personal eating habits up for what they are.

Anyway, we whipped the three or four blocks to Dolly's to grub down before starting our day in the learning machine. Elaine met us there like she always does. She has the same aversion to 5:30 in the morning that Max does, so she only works out in the afternoons. Elaine was national caliber in the 'fly and distance freestyle, a fairly unusual combination, but she doesn't compete anymore, like I said. One thing about swimming: unless you're among the best in the country, there's a girl somewhere who can kick your butt—any stroke, any distance. Elaine was that girl for a lot of guys around here; she had her day, but no more. Elaine swims for fun.

So the four of us are at Dolly's, buried in a Disneyland of pancakes, eggs, bacon, hashbrowns, toast and Nortie's bowl of raisins and rice, and poor old Nortie can't get Stotan Week off his pea brain.

"What do you think it is, Walk?" There is an urgency in his voice that does not become a man of his physical capabilities, squirrelly as he may appear.

"Don't whine, peckerneck," Jeff says. "You're a hero in this high school; an aquatic phenom. Don't whine."

I've got a soft spot for Nortie, but I'll be damned if I know how he's going to survive his first twenty-four hours after graduation. I mean, he's eighteen years old. People will soon expect him to be an adult. I say, "I don't know what it is, Nort, but it won't be fun; at least not in the conventional sense."

"Think it's gonna be really tough, huh?"

Nortie's strange. He works out as hard as anyone on the team, maybe harder, but anticipation short-circuits him. It breaks my heart, but I say, "Yes, Nort. I think it will be really tough."

Lion says, "Did you see the *look* on Max? *I* think it will be tough."

Nortie groans.

Elaine plops a chair down at the end of the table at our booth and punches Nortie lightly on the shoulder. "Norton," she says, "you look distressed. What's the matter, baby?"

"Stotan Week," he says. "We're having Stotan Week."

Jeff puts down his fork for the first time since we sat down. "It's voluntary, for Chrissakes, Nortie. That means you go only if you want to. And, Nortie, you don't even know what it is, so will you please shut up? You're driving me nuts and I feel like I may have to kill you." Though Jeff loves Nortie like a brother, he's a little less indulgent of him than the rest of us.

Nortie nods and is quiet. He knows Jeff is kidding, sort of, but he doesn't mess with him.

Elaine is psyched out of her gourd because she and some other cosmic wizards from Frost have been invited to take an Astronomy course at Gonzaga U. for college credit and they get to use the school's planetarium, and I have to say, if anyone I know would be at home in a planetarium, it's Elaine.

Her first class was last night; she doesn't want to talk about Stotan Week. "Don't Time and Space just freak you out?" she offers up to any takers. There are none. Time freaks most of us out—everything we do is against the clock.

Elaine is undaunted by Jeff's eyes rolling back and Nortie's head cocking like a confused cocker spaniel's.

"Did you know that most of the stars we see could be burned out by the time we see them?" she asks.

"Really?" Jeff asks in mock horror. He squints and points his fork. "Deep meaning here, right? You're going to tell us who changes them when they burn out."

Elaine points back and raises her eyebrows. "Things may not be as they appear to be, O wise carrot-top. Beware."

"Is that my horoscope for November 5, Omar?" Jeff says.

Elaine smiles her smug little smile and takes a drink of Jeff's orange juice. "You'll see," she says. "You'll all see."

Elaine takes a lot of crap from the rest of us about her perception of what we're doing on this planet, and she gives out a fair share too, but underneath—and not very far underneath—she's dead serious in her quest for other-than-traditional knowledge. We figure she'll go to college next year and major in Weirdness. I mean, besides the Astronomy class, she's signed up for a night course from Eastern Washington U. called Tibetan Symbolism, and last year she took something called Applied Concepts of Karma in the Western World. Jeff tells her if she keeps it up he can get her a full ride to Rod Serling University. Boy, she can make your head swim in a philosophical discussion; make you wonder what's real—what's important.

I may not know what's important in the universal sense, but I know what's important to me right now, and that's finishing out this year with a bang. I want to swim fast and help my buddies swim fast—make the last year of swimming at Frost one they'll remember. I also want to do a good job with my studies for once, to prove myself, so I don't head off to college next year with my return-trip ticket already bought. I think I might be pretty smart, but that's gone untested from a scholastic point of view, because I think I'm also pretty lazy. I've been working to correct that, though. In my attempt to become semi-literate I even read a few books cover-to-cover this last summer, and though it's not MTV, it's not half bad. I could get into being a student, with a little practice. See, I have a brother who's fifteen years older than me floating around town, and, to hear him tell it, he was a pretty smart cookie. He's forever giving me books to read, and old sixties record albums to listen to so that I can, according to him, improve my mind and become cultured in the way of the old masters—the Hippies. I worry about my brother a little, though. He never got cut loose from that time. I mean, even Jerry Rubin and Abbie Hoffman moved on. And Tom Hayden is a respected politician in California these days, and not just because he has the good sense to lust after Jane Fonda's body. But my brother—his name's Long John—still puts drugs into every orifice he can find and preaches love and non-violence like he was gathering followers for a migration to Woodstock. Unfortunately, I'm afraid he's a pusher. He has no visible means of support, and though he never has a lot of material things, he never goes hungry either. If I ever find out that's true for sure, he and I may well have a parting of the ways, but meantime I read his books and listen to his music and learn what I can from him.

CHAPTER 2

November 12

Nortie volunteered for Stotan Week today. The little screwball hoped Max would tell him more about it if he just walked in and signed up, but Max merely said okay and wrote his name down. Now he's begging the rest of us to hurry and go volunteer so he won't have to go through it alone; and we all will, of course, but not before we terrorize his scrawny butt a few more days.

His panic is becoming full-blown. "C'mon, you guys. Hurry and sign up. You're not going to let me go alone, are you? God, just me and Max? I wouldn't last five minutes. What *is* it? I tried to look it up in the dictionary, but there's no 'Stotan'; not even in the big one in the library." It doesn't matter that Max has never thrown a workout at us Nortie couldn't take. We keep telling him that we're going to be out of town that week or that you'd have to be an idiot to volunteer for something when you don't know anything about it. Part of it's an act, but he'll rest a lot easier when our signatures are on the paper. We won't let it go on much longer, mostly because we don't want a major gastric disorder to be visited on our fastest swimmer.

The only thing Max has said since he put up the notice last week is that Stotan Week will require total commitment.

Lion's up for it. He trusts Max to come up with something to equal all this drama, and to Lion that means a chance to extend himself—which is what he does best. Lion and Elaine are alike in that respect.

What Lion is, first, is an artist. When he's not swimming or in class, he's making pictures. I don't know much about art—I don't even know what I like—but I don't have to sit in the cafeteria or out in the hills along the Little Spokane River watching him sketch for long to know he has a boatload of talent and, I think, probably the personality and arrogance to stretch it as far as it will go. Mark my words: you'll be hearing from Lionel Serbousek.

His art isn't just picture-making, though. Lion's an artist at everything he does. He brings a certain zany grace to things—workouts, classes, just hanging out—that makes them more alive, more animated, maybe more real. He's long been legendary around Frost for his madcap hijinks, like the time he set the school record for snorting Jell-O cubes. Lion's different from the rest of us because he doesn't have parents. They got killed in a freak boating accident over on Coeur d'Alene Lake between our freshman and sophomore years, when their boat and another speedboat collided at full speed out in the middle of the lake. No one ever figured out how it happened; they weren't drinking or anything, and they'd been boating all their lives. Everybody in both boats was killed. Lion didn't have anyplace to go—no relatives or anything—and he

11

didn't feel like moving in with any of the people who offered, so he got himself an apartment, if you can call it that, and started living by himself. I don't know whether that's legal or not, but nobody stopped him. His folks had plenty of life insurance and he inherited some other money from them, so he doesn't have to work to support himself. Most of the time he goes on like nothing happened.

We've talked about staying together for Stotan Week—that is, when Nortie's not around to hear we all know we're going to sign up—and have decided if our folks will let us, we'll move into Lion's for the week. Now, I said Lion was an artist at everything he does, but in his personal lifestyle that holds true only if you're looking for Still Life of Swine. His so-called apartment is two condemned rooms above the Fireside Tavern with a bed, a hotplate, a sink that drains out onto an alley and—the one really class item—a toilet with a seat belt. He's got a seat belt on his toilet. Claims it keeps him from blasting off. There are no electric lights in this palatial suite, and the sole source of heat is an old electric reflector heater powered by a frayed extension cord running out the window and down to the outlet behind the bar in the Fireside. Artificial light, lest you think these quarters uncivilized, shines from a flashlight dangling at the end of a rope above his bed.

I would like to go on record here—despite the sense of adventure for doing this Stotan Week thing together on our own—that I am not looking forward to spending a week with the guys in Lionel Serbousek's bachelor pad.

Besides voluntarily placing myself in ghetto-like accommodations at Lion's, the only thing that really bothers me about Stotan Week is that I was looking forward, during this extra week at Christmas, to spending some time with my brother. I said he was a little out of touch and that's probably the understatement of this decade. It's strange how I feel responsible for him sometimes—I mean, we were never really close or anything. He was off to college by the time I was five, and pretty well into the flower world not long after that. He was always nice to me when he was around, but, given his political leanings, he and my dad weren't famous friends, so he wasn't around all that much. But, for whatever reason, I feel protective of him like he's a stray errant uncle or something; I'm always making excuses for the weird way he acts and the stupid choices he makes. One of these days my concern for him may get me killed, or at least seriously mangled. He spends a lot of time over at the Red Rooster Tavern, drinking beer and buying drugs from the bikers who hang out there. I shouldn't have to go into a detailed description to let you know that's a rough scene. My folks have given up on him, so when he gets in trouble it's me who bails him out. When he goes off the deep end, Ed Savage, one of the bartenders over at the Rooster, calls me to come get him, instead of calling the police or someone from the looney bin. I don't know how that little ritual got started, and there are times I feel like letting the law haul him off, but I always go. And I want to tell you, it's scary over there. I went to get him one night the summer before my sophomore year, and eight or nine of those bikers had him stuffed in a garbage can up on the pool table—butt first, so his feet and head were sticking out—and they were spitting snoose at him for target practice. When I tried to get him down, they kept right on spitting. Ed had to threaten to call the cops to get them to let me out of there with him. One of them grabbed my arm on the way out and let me know Long John owed him money for "goods received" and if I came down there again to get him, I damn well better be able to pay off his debts. I was so scared I lied and said I would, that I'd get the money he owed them by the end of the week, and he slapped me a couple of times hard on the cheek, squinted and smiled and nodded his head. When I got Long John back to his room at the Jefferson Hotel, he told me what a great brother I was and he was glad I understood. I understood diddly. I screamed at him that he'd almost got me killed and I never wanted to see him again, and if he got into any more trouble he could sit it out in jail, if he was lucky enough to have someone call the cops. Then I went home and lay in bed and trembled. I got over hating him, but I didn't get over the terror I felt about those bikers. No doubt they'd as soon tear off my head and spit in the hole as look at me. I decided then and there I was going to make it risky to mess with me. Next day I went into Max's office and asked if he could have me transferred into the karate section of PE. He started me out there, and worked with me some on his own; didn't even ask what I was up to. He also got me a key to the wrestling room, where the class is held, and said I could practice any time I wanted as long as it wasn't being used. He gave me some drills to work on too, and I've been putting in a couple hours a day at least five days a week since then. I'm not a mean guy and I never go out looking, but even though I haven't passed any tests and I don't have any "belts," I've developed some pretty classy moves and, if it comes down to it, I can hurt you.

From the sound of all the tough talk, you'd think all I do is try to go fast in the water and strike fear in the hearts of those who cross my path, but that's not true at all. I no longer have any illusions of single-handedly cleaning out a biker bar, and the stuff with Long John is really peripheral to what's important to me. I'm part of a group of really special guys—and a girl—who happen to swim, and I'm a little paranoid about being physically vulnerable, but it's a lot more important to me to be a part of that group of humans than it is to be in a school of fast fish or to flaunt a truckload of Billy Jack moves. We all know this is it for the frivolous part of our lives; we're going to have to go out and start the real thing very soon. We want to do that with style, and we want to finish this part together.

You have probably figured out by now, if you can count, that my parents are old people. Figure my brother is fifteen years older than me, and my parents got a late start anyway—that puts them right up there. Old people call my parents old. They're older than lots of my friends' grandparents. Folks used to rub my head and tease me about how lucky I was that my rambunctious daddy saved up enough rugged sperms to produce such a healthy specimen as myself, and Dad used to laugh and shake his head when he heard it, but I have a feeling he would have just as soon not had to deal with a brand-new bouncing baby boy at the ripe old age of fifty-five. There was no way either of my folks was ready to spend another eighteen years practicing the latest child-rearing techniques. So they kind of let me raise myself. Don't get me wrong, they have always been good to me and pretty much given me everything I need and most of what I want, but they're not very involved with me. I don't think I've suffered much, though, because, even though Max is a little removed, in a lot of ways he's been as good a parent as I could ask for.

It's kind of scary sometimes to think that we'll all go our own ways after this year—break up this little group that has really been together since grade school. None of us is fool enough to think that we can keep things like this forever, but there are times I'd really like to give it a try. Nortie and I will probably get swimming scholarships somewhere, maybe together and maybe not, and Jeff will more than likely follow his girlfriend down to Stanford, where she's a freshman this year. God, he's in love with her! He'll probably major in Political Science just so he can spend the rest of his life telling folks how things really are.

And who knows about Lion? He's fast becoming Frost's Renaissance man; commie pinko in the a.m., imperialist pig after lunch. He fools around with ideas for the sake of fooling around; tries them on, wears them a few hours, swearing they are a part of his very soul, then casts them off like he should cast off his old sweatsocks, but doesn't. His most intense beliefs are lightly held, and he changes philosophical positions like a chameleon changes hues. Ten years from now Lion could show up just about anywhere and I wouldn't be surprised. I would only be surprised if he doesn't show up.

If Nortie doesn't become a permanent orphan some-where, he'll more than likely be a grade-school teacher. He loves little kids; talks to them on their own level—which I sometimes think is his own level. Nortie works a few nights a week and Saturdays at a daycare center over on the east side, where most of the town's blacks live. Boy, he's amaz-ing. It's a completely different Nortie; I've seen him work. He knows what makes little kids tick, where their pain is and how to help them fly. Given his Catholic background, he'll probably teach at St. Somebody's school, which means he'll never be rich—but he'll be happy as a pig in mud if he can spend his time making their lives better. Old Nortie has a lot of heart.

Me, I'd like to be a writer of some kind; maybe a jour-nalist, maybe a storyteller. I should have my choice of at least a few schools once this swimming season is over, and I think I'll pick the one with the best English and Journalism departments. I love to write things down, be they fact or fiction. It helps me see things more clearly, and besides I just enjoy it. That's why I have a semi-regular column in the school newspaper, even though I'm not in the Journalism class, and why I submit articles to the *Spokesman Review* and the Sunday supplement. I've actually had one or two published. I used to go out with a girl whose dad was a bigwig at the *Review,* and even though the relationship was a marathon screaming match, he liked me and still throws a few bones my way when they need some local public-school filler. I was afraid that would stop when I quit going out with his daughter, but he told me recently it would have stopped if I'd *kept* going out with his daughter.

November 13

Nortie and I were over at my place this afternoon after workout, up in my room listening to some music and pretending to get some study time in, when Jeff came a-pounding on the door. We were lying there on the beds listening to an old Kingston Trio album (part of the cultural legacy left me by Long John Dupree), helping them out now and then with a little burst of the lyrics and flipping through the pages of our U.S. Government book like we might be learning something. Jeff had a very old *Sports Illustrated* he'd obviously lifted from the city library rolled up in his hand, and the grin of a man in the catbird seat. "Hi, Anus Breath," he said. "I have some good news and some bad news."

"Give me the good news," I said. "You can keep the bad news to yourself."

"The good news," he said with a grandiose sweeping gesture of the magazine, "is your hero now knows what a Stotan is," and he pointed to the magazine. He shook his head and looked to the heavens. "God, redheads are bright. Do you know the average SAT score for redheads as opposed to the rest of mankind?"

The question passed over Nortie as he laid his book aside and sat up. "So what's the bad news?" he asked. "Give us the bad news."

"The bad news is," Jeff said, his grin widening considerably, "I found out what a Stotan is." He shook his head. "It isn't pretty."

Nortie groaned and sat back against the wall. "Oh, God," he moaned. "What is it?"

Jeff said, "You don't want to know. I will tell you this much. The term was coined somewhere after the middle of this very century in Australia. Further knowledge can be obtained by interested parties through clandestine arrangements for sexual favors with family members—preferably mothers and sisters." He did an exaggerated about-face and high-stepped out of the room.

Nortie was up in an instant, following him out, yelling, "Wait, Jeff! You can sleep with *my* sister." It's a good thing my parents weren't home.

Jeff has an abscessed front tooth with a temporary hole drilled in the back for drainage, and the substance that comes out would be more appropriate draining into the alley behind Lion's apartment than into someone's mouth— even Jeff's. It drains very slowly—it's been like that for months, with no end in sight according to his dentist—so he doesn't have the taste all the time, but when he wants to he can suck it out with his tongue, blow it on you and flatten you out. I've always said if any of us could take Max and his black belt, it would be Jeff and his magic tooth. Max would get one whiff and kick his own brains out trying to get out of his misery.

Nortie ran back into the room with a stunned expression and a tear in his eye.

"Any luck?" I asked.

Nortie gasped. "He knows I don't have a sister." He wiped his eye. "Jeez, why does he do that? He sucked his tooth."

CHAPTER 3

November 14

You have to hurt a little for Nortie. He's a classic case of what can happen to a guy who's been beat up all his life. Eighteen years old and his old man still punches him around.

I've asked Nort why he doesn't just kiss him off—tell him to go to hell and stay with me for the rest of the year— but he shrugs and says his dad's okay; he just doesn't know any other way to act. I tell him it's time he *learned* some other way to act or to hell with him, but Nortie dodges that.

When we were sophomores, I went to their place for dinner one Sunday afternoon just before Christmas. I think Nortie was uncomfortable having someone come over because his dad can be so ornery and unpredictable, but he had eaten at my place so many times he figured it was time to take a chance. Anyway, right before dinner, around three in the afternoon, Nortie and I jumped in their family car to run over to the local 7–11 to get whipped cream for the pie, and as we were pulling out of the parking lot, some guy slid around the corner on the ice and slammed into our front fender. There was absolutely no way Nortie could have prevented it—in fact, we were stopped when the guy hit us—but Nortie got real quiet, sort of set his jaw, and after they exchanged insurance information, we drove home.

His dad happened to see us drive up out the living-room window and was barreling down the sidewalk toward us before Nortie could even get out. He jerked Nortie out of the car onto his hands and knees, then lifted him up and slapped the sides of his head, screaming at him. When Nortie put his hands up to protect his head, his dad gave him a hard shot to the solar plexus and dropped him. To this day I'm embarrassed that I didn't jump out of the car and take my best shot at Mr. Wheeler, but I sat frozen, my eyes glued to his face. He isn't a very big guy, but he looked *so* mean, deliberately aiming each of his shots. When Nortie hit the ground, I came unfrozen; jumped out and ran around the car to help him up. His wind was gone and he was convulsing for air, but he waved me away. His dad was yelling, "Let the little screw be! I'll teach him to mess up my car!"

I tried to explain what had happened, that it wasn't Nortie's fault, but I couldn't make him hear me. Mr. Wheeler has Nortie pegged for a screw-up, and the facts be damned.

Nortie's mom watched it all out the living-room window and she didn't move a muscle. For a quick second I remember hating her guts, but later I thought of the times I'd seen her wearing sunglasses on dark days and long sleeves on hot days to cover up her own bruises, and I guessed she was doing what she had to to get along. Still, it's hard to respect her.

I didn't stay for dinner.

Boy, it's no wonder that little turd is so fast. He's just a demon in workouts. He's so nervous before every practice he can't eat lunch and he whines and bitches and moans like a third-grader on Death Row as 2:30 approaches, but when we hit the water, he pays the pool back for every time his old man ever laid a finger on him. I hope he finds an outlet when we're through with swimming, because he's got to have a lot of mean energy boiling around in him.

I think I'd like to get the whole truth about Stotan Week from Max because Max is a human being, but I have a feeling I'm going to get it from Jeff, who isn't. I found a note on my desk in English class today—about an hour after he tried to assassinate Nortie again in the hall with a blast from his chemical breath because Nortie had the audacity to try to get him to cough up Stotan information for free. The note said, "Learn all you can about Herb Elliot." It wasn't signed, but I'd recognize Jeff's handwriting anywhere. It looks like he dipped the feet of a baby chick in ink, placed it on the page and set the little bugger ablaze. Big as he is on current events, Jeff's a researching fool. You could have bet he'd be the one to crack this Stotan mystery, but you could also count on his not telling anyone what he found out. I do know who Herb Elliot is, so that's a start.

November 15

Being the serious-minded student of current affairs he is, Jeff has appointed himself Frost's official unofficial political analyst and at times he bowls you over with it. If you want the real reasons the Russians boycotted the Olympics, or the hot poop on the sudden unexplained disappearance of one unnamed assistant football coach and one similarly unnamed cheerleader, Jeff's your man. For local, national and regional news, see Jeffrey Hawkins in flaming red color at six and eleven. Of course, he delivers each newsy tidbit like it's the Russian invasion of Afghanistan or the release of the Iranian hostages, so some analysis on your own part is in order, but he's a smart motor scooter and he does his homework. You're making a mistake if you don't listen to what he has to say, no matter how obnoxious he makes it.

"Up for a little racial tension?" he asked me in the lunch line today. He showed up with Lion and Elaine, armed to the teeth with Doomsday warnings. Yesterday, Herb Elliot. Today, racial tension. The man has range.

"Sure, I haven't got a lot else to think about," I said, looking at Elaine and Lion, then back to Walter Cronkite. "What week is *that* scheduled for?"

"Coming soon to a theater near you," he said, reached inside his coat and pulled out a rolled-up newspaper, unrolled it and spread it out on my tray. I put a plate of burgers—one dish the nutritional demolition squad in the cafeteria hasn't yet learned to destroy—on top of it. The girl behind the counter informed me that there was a two-burger limit. I've been eating here once a day for the last four years and that rule has always been the same on burger day. "Really?" I said. "Sorry, I didn't know that." I put the rest back and, when she looked the other way, slipped an extra under my coat. I tell you, it's a never ending battle.

We moved out into the dining area, over by a window, and set our trays on a table. Lion opened his bookbag and removed a Mason jar and a Tupperware container that he filled with milk and peanut butter respectively, for later consumption. There is no late-night food service in his palatial digs like there is in homes with regular families, so he stocks up in the cafeteria. Once when one of the guys who cleans the tables in the cafeteria told him he couldn't be taking food off the premises, Lion told him it was okay, that he was one of three athletes in the nation who'd been awarded athletic scholarships to high school, and there was an "all you can eat" clause in his. That's the last that was said. No one messes much with Lion. The kindest thing said about his presentation of himself is it's "different" and that's not the half of it; and he's a real horse. Except for maybe Jeff, he's the biggest guy I've ever seen call himself a swimmer. We are not talking svelte and streamlined here. These are guys who, when we're up to 10,000 to 12,000 yards a day and their percentage of body fat is zero or less, still weigh in around 190. Lion and Jeff do not look like the swimmers you see atop the Olympic podium; Lion and Jeff are chiseled out of marble block with crude tools. These are not sleek sailboats; these are destroyers.

I removed the paper from under my plate and gave it a look. It was called the *Aryan Press* and in the center of the front page was a not very professional drawing of an ape alongside an equal-quality drawing of a black man. Both were side profiles in similar positions, bent forward and staring straight ahead. Around each picture were labels and arrows showing assumed similarities between the two. I've seen it before on a poster—though more professionally drawn—down in the men's can at the Red Rooster. It's the "scientific proof" bigots use to prove blacks are further back on the evolutionary scale than whites. If it weren't so silly, it'd be downright offensive. The rest of the paper was filled with stories about atrocities Jews and blacks have committed on the blue-eyed, blond population through the ages—a couple of hard shots to the stomach about "equal opportunity" and some serious warnings about the dangers of contaminating a pure bloodline. I stared at it a few seconds, then asked Jeff where he got it.

"They're all over school," he said. "Somebody's been sticking them in unlocked lockers, and there's a stack of them out by the front entrance."

Before any of us could say what we thought we should do, Lion was up and headed for the door. Jeff and Elaine and I followed him out of sheer habit. At the front entrance he took one look at the stack of papers, moved them to the middle of the sidewalk, broke the bailing wire that held them together, spread them out a little for air and put a match to them. The match blew out and he tried another. Someone threw him a disposable lighter and that did the trick. Without thinking, we were into the spirit, moving the metal garbage cans around the fire to keep it contained, and stood watching the papers burn as kids and teachers poured out of classrooms and the cafeteria. Most of them obviously didn't know what the commotion was about, and Lion passed a couple of unburned copies among them. Then he stood up on one of the garbage cans and raised his hands. He presented enough of a spectacle to get something that vaguely resembled silence, and he roared, "I catch anyone passing this crap out and he'll answer to me for it! I'll kick his butt! I've been going to this school four years and I'm proud of it! This crap stinks and I won't have it!" He got down as Mrs. Stevens, the vice-principal, stormed through the doors with a fire extinguisher. She extinguished the flames in seconds, then turned to the crowd, furious. "Who's responsible for this?" she demanded, and Lion stepped forward.

"I am," he said, "and I'm headed for your office."

Mrs. Stevens said, "You better be, Buster, and you better have a darn good explanation." They both disappeared as Elaine and Jeff and I started picking up the partially burned papers, cramming them into the garbage drums. I felt a hand on my shoulder and turned to see Max. "What's going on?" he asked, and I handed him one of the papers. He looked at it and smiled, shaking his head. "Lion find a cause?" he asked.

I smiled and nodded. "Looks like it."

Max shook his head again and said, "I wouldn't give it my time." He went back inside.

It had all happened so fast no one had time to think. That's the way Lion is. When he's hot, he comes on like a flash flood. He knows exactly what his values are at any given moment and what he's willing to go to the wall for; let the consequences fall into place later. Consequences would be light for this. Lion would be back in the cafeteria almost before we would. Mrs. Stevens came to Frost seven years ago because she's been the most successful administrator in the city at taking care of racial issues, and though there aren't all that many blacks in Spokane, Frost has by far the majority of them.

Mrs. Stevens is black.

We weren't back in the cafeteria five minutes before Lion was there, stuffing his face as though nothing had happened. "Can't let that stuff get out of hand," he said. "Boy, I like that Mrs. Stevens."

I looked to Jeff. "Well, I guess that takes care of racial tension," I said.

He shrugged and raised his eyebrows. "We'll see," he said. "You know, those are printed locally, over in Falls Lake. Those guys have been there quite a while, but it looks like they're trying to get something started. You'd be surprised how many people believe that crap even though they're not in the inner circle."

Lion took another huge bite and said, "I better not see any more of them."

Elaine got up to get another burger and I remember feeling a little self-conscious about watching her butt move toward the counter like the flanks of a thoroughbred racehorse. Old Elaine wears some fairly tight britches and she's real muscular. She's always been one of the guys, so it feels a little like incest, but she's been wedging herself into my dreams lately, and there's not much a guy can do about that. That's not information I'm ready to put out for group discussion, but that's the way it is. It doesn't help that I already have a girlfriend.

"So tell me, O wise red peckerhead," I said to Jeff, in a futile effort to banish Elaine from my lunchtime fantasies, "what's today's little teaser on Stotan Week?"

"You didn't check out Herb Elliot, did you?"

I had to admit I hadn't.

"I have to know you really *want* this information, Walk," he said. "I just can't give it out. I have to feel needed."

Elaine sat down again. "A Stotan is a cross between a Stoic and a Spartan," she said, and Jeff's chin dropped to his pecs. "The term was coined by Percy Cerruti, coach of the great Australian miler Herb Elliot in the late fifties and early sixties." She ran it off with encyclopedic brilliance. "Cerruti used that term to describe Elliot in his single-minded determination to be the greatest miler of all time. Elliot would do his regular workouts, which were considerable, then throw off his clothes to run dune after dune on the Australian beaches, driving himself to the brink of exhausted ecstasy. Herb Elliot thought American athletes were wussies. Percy Cerruti thought Herb Elliot was a Stotan." She chomped down on her burger.

"Slime-bag," Jeff said. "Scuzz-ball."

Elaine went on, seemingly delighted by Jeff's epithet. "I would imagine that Stotan Week will be a week in which Max asks you to put forth Stotanic efforts to make yourselves less like wussies and more like Herb Elliot."

Lion's eyes lit up; you could see his mind whipping along ahead of Elaine, visions of himself and Herb charging over an infinity of Australian sand dunes, then diving into the surf and swimming to New Zealand.

Jeff was pissed at having been scooped.

CHAPTER 4

November 23

Well, Thanksgiving was yesterday and I have a pound or two to swim off. It shouldn't be too bad, though. We went over to the pool in the morning and put in about 4,000 yards before going home and putting in about 4,000 calories. Actually, I didn't do that at my home. I did it at Elaine's. That's right, this smooth captain wangled an invite to her place for Thanksgiving dinner and didn't even do a whole lot of damage to his relationship with his parents in the process. My folks had planned for several months to go to my dad's sister's place in Seattle for Thanksgiving and I was able to convince them that if I didn't work out Thursday and Friday I'd lose too much to make up. Mom and Dad know next to nothing about swimming—in fact, I can't remember them going to a meet—but they know it's important to me, and in the interest of letting me do and have anything I want, they let me beg off going to Seattle. Letting my orphan status out in the presence of Elaine's mother was no difficult task either, so I ended up right where I wanted to be. It was probably a bad idea for my libido, but I couldn't pass it up. I don't think there's a way to take care of this. In my wildest imagination I can't see me telling Elaine I'm hot for her. If she did believe me, she'd punch me in the nose. She's a tough one, that Elaine. It's also going to be hard to explain to Devnee, my supposed girlfriend, why, with my parents out of town for the holiday, I didn't spend it with her. Probably what I'll do with that is lie. I've got to stop that one of these days—it seems like I lie pretty easily and convincingly to girls—but not right now. I've got my hands full figuring out how crazy I am even thinking about Elaine. Boy, I hope this stuff with girls gets easier when you get older. So far it's a big pain in the butt.

Under any circumstances Elaine and I are good friends, and dinner was really nice. Her mom is one of those people you'd adopt as a parent, given the choice. In fact, back in our AAU swimming days, when she drove us to all the meets, I thought she *was* my mother. She's a big, strong, smart, earthy woman with a huge heart and it's a treat to be around her. If she has a fault, however, it's her taste in men. You have to meet Elaine's dad to believe him. Elaine's been telling stories about him for years, and from what I saw yesterday, nothing has changed. The man's a pack rat—a collector. The nooks and crannies of the house are filled with cases of canned food, scuba tanks, old car parts, an old plow blade, for Chrissakes, and enough telephone parts to start a medium-sized communication company. His holdings are much expanded from last time I was there. When I asked him what it was all for, he just smiled and said you never know when you might need some of that stuff. I pictured a flash flood where Mr. Ferral fights his way through the crashing wall of water raging through the kitchen, straps on his scuba tank and makes himself a telephone to call for help, thereby saving his entire family, which is cowering behind the plow blade for protection from the canned goods washing through the room.

And he never leaves the couch. He lives on the couch. He has two TV sets within arm's reach and Elaine says the only way on earth to get his attention is to walk in front of one of them. They're both going all the time and they're set on different channels, the sound up on only one. He switches them back and forth at will, and I guarantee it'll drive you stark raving berserk to watch a program with him. The master stroke in all this, however, is an adjustable, wide-angle rearview mirror mounted on the back of the couch. When I first saw it, several years ago, I thought it was just another of the legion of bizarre items strewn around the house, but when I accidentally bumped it, it didn't fall over. It's screwed right down into the frame so he can watch TV from either side.

"It doesn't bother you that the titles come up backward, I guess," I said.

"The human mind is a wonderful thing," he said. "It can get used to almost anything. The Chinese read like that all the time."

I don't think that's exactly how the Chinese read, but I got the point.

I stayed quite a ways into the evening and Elaine and I went for a walk around her neighborhood. Except for their house, which would be a blight on the poorest sections of Newark, New Jersey, because of all the junk Mr. Ferral has piled around, seemingly holding the house up, the neighborhood is a nice, quiet little lower-middle-class place with a comfortable feeling of families who have lived their whole lives there. We live in a ritzier part of town that feels sterile to me. I know our nextdoor neighbors, but I don't know any of the people up and down the street. Elaine's neighborhood is like a little community.

The leaves on the trees are nearly gone and temperatures have been getting down around freezing at night, so smoke curled out of almost every chimney and it felt like there was probably a lot in that little neighborhood to be thankful for. It seemed as if Elaine and I bumped gently together a few times more than random chance would have it, but it's hard to say. I was pretty aware. We talked about swimming and what it would take for me to do well at State—how much I wanted it—and a little about the Nazi newspapers that Lion burned, and about how strange it seems to me sometimes that I'm so far away from my parents and that my brother is like a distant uncle to me unless we have a reason to purposely make a connection. Sometimes I wonder who I am, because it seems like I don't have a solid anchor in my family. Elaine said she thought when we don't have a family to hook up to, we hook up to the next-best thing—our friends. "Look at Lion," she said. "He doesn't have any family at all, but he knows who he is, mostly in relationship to all of us. You probably do that some too."

"I know I do," I said. "And, all in all, it's probably more healthy than what my real family has to offer. But I keep getting pulled back to them. I want my brother to be different. I want his life to mean something. And, Christ, just because my parents are old doesn't mean they have to give up on everything. Sometimes I think they're just breathing our air. My family doesn't have any *personality*."

She smiled. "They aren't exactly the Beaver Cleavers, but they could be worse. You could have *my* dad. Look at the things *he* makes important." She shrugged. "You have to go with what you get."

We got back to the house and Elaine made me a monstrous turkey sandwich and wrapped a piece of pumpkin pie for later. Her mom invited me back for the meal of my choice over the weekend, but I politely declined, telling her I might need it more later; that I'd take a rain check. It was after midnight when I turned onto the arterial leading up onto the South Hill, where I live. It was one of those times when I felt closer to getting a better look at things. Talking with Elaine like that, with no judgment from her or anything, seemed to bring my feelings more to the surface so I could look at them. I love times like that; you don't get many of them. I passed the turn-off to our house and continued on up to 57th and out to the Palouse Highway, which heads east toward the Idaho panhandle. There wasn't another car on the road and the white line shooting under my car had an almost hypnotic effect. Away from town, the stars became bright enough to outline the mountains around me, and I turned off the dash lights and leaned over the steering wheel to look up at the Milky Way. Out there alone, it was a lot easier to see why Elaine gets such a charge out of her Astronomy class. I must have driven for an hour and a half in my little Duster cocoon, thinking; trying to come up with answers for the things I think are important. I came up with a lot more questions than answers: like, what am I going to do about Devnee, my girlfriend? She's a nice girl—a really pretty girl—who I've been going with about two months longer than I should have, obviously, because I don't feel anything for her anymore; but I can't say that to her. I just can't do it—no matter how much I want to end it and no matter how much I have to fake it when we're making out. When the moment comes to say, "I just don't care about you anymore," or whatever I could come up with, I just cannot do it. Does that mean I have to marry her?

33

And how about old Long John? Somehow he gets me thinking that because our parents don't have time for him anymore—or at least Dad doesn't—that responsibility has fallen to me. I admit I get some interesting information from him, and sometimes he's fun to be around because he's smart and funny, but he's also a drug freak who won't take care of his own life and has caused me maximum grief. And I think he could take from me forever, and he will if I don't stop him.

My mind drifted along the lines of Elaine's and my conversation and came up with zero conclusions, which has been standard lately for this aquatic Aristotle.

With not one clear resolution, I finally turned the car around and headed for home.

CHAPTER 5

November 29

It's too bad this school wasn't named after Jim Thorpe or Jackie Robinson or some other great athlete, rather than a poet or a snowman. I mean, Frost is a jock school. You don't have a lot of pull if you're a swimmer, because swimming is on the way out and it's not the world's most exciting spectator sport anyway. It's hardly engrossing to watch six mostly naked guys motor from one end of the pool to the other as fast as they can, only to turn around and go back. But the coaches and jocks in the major sports are hot stuff around here and they have a lot of influence. That's because Frost has good teams in the major sports. We win a *lot* of athletic contests every year and get a lot of play in the local papers. The Athletic Council, made up of the captains of each team and the coaches of the major sports, is probably more influential than the Student Council, mostly because the Student Body President is also the captain of the basketball team and is *the* consummate jock. In this school, jocks rule.

This is my third year as captain of the swim team, so I've been on the Council since I was a sophomore. In those three years, up until last week, I don't remember a time when the Athletic Council wasn't unanimous on any decision or opinion we made. I think that's because Mr. Edwards, the football coach, and Mr. Severs, the baseball coach, are big, strong, imposing men who state their opinions, fold their arms and silently dare you to go against them. They don't do that to be bad guys, it's just the way they are. Even if you didn't agree with them, which most of us usually do, you'd have to be a strong believer in the other side to take them on. And you'd lose.

I bring that up only because the meeting this last week was the first time I ever remember any of us at odds on an issue that didn't get worked out, Edwards and Severs or no Edwards and Severs. And it was about that stupid *Aryan Press*. That's like arguing over an article in the *National Enquirer*.

A girl named Molly Ramstead, who's on the girls' basketball team, moved that the Council issue a public statement against the stuff in the *Aryan Press* in case there was the slightest doubt in anybody's mind that *anyone* in this school agrees with that crap. There are two black kids on the Council, Roy Biggs from the track team and LaFesha Stills from girls' softball. They just smiled and looked at the table, shaking their heads. I couldn't tell what they were thinking, probably that we were ridiculous for even wasting time with it, but I seconded Molly's motion and added that we should approach the administration about taking disciplinary action against anyone distributing it.

And that's what started it. Marty O'Brian, who's the rep from the baseball team, a catcher whose marvelous athletic talents are surpassed only by his monumental insensitivity, said, "That's against the Constitution."

"What constitution is that?" I asked. I couldn't *believe* we'd have trouble passing this.

"The Constitution of the United States. Freedom of the press. Freedom of speech."

I've never liked O'Brian much anyway, if for no other reason than he's an opinionated, arrogant turdburger who's always tormenting Nortie about swimming being a sissy sport, and I welcomed the opportunity to take him on. "Who read that to you?" I asked. "You pick that up your second time through Civics?"

"People are entitled to an opinion," he said. "The law says so. Just because you don't agree with it doesn't mean you can wipe it out. That's what the commies do."

I was getting hot because I didn't like that peckerwood calling me a commie and because he was winning the argument already and because he makes me sick. I said, "Maybe the law should say people need to keep some opinions to themselves."

"Maybe it should, but it doesn't." For once in his life O'Brian was making sense and I hated it. I was on thin Constitutional ice and I knew it. I mean, the ACLU is forever sticking up for the Klan and the John Birchers and every other jerk-off organization the bigots of our great land can hide behind. So I decided to see if I could pin old Marty down a little—maybe make him say something racist that the black kids could take back to their friends and get him roughed up a little.

"So what's your beef, Marty?" I said. "If we take the part out about disciplinary action against any distributors, you willing to make a unanimous statement against that rag?"

Marty hesitated too long before saying, "Yeah, sure."

Roy and LaFesha picked up on it too, but they just smiled and looked at the table again. When we finally took the vote on the statement only, O'Brian changed his mind and abstained. He said it was to keep me humble, but I had to ask. "Marty," I said, "were you the guy that brought those papers in?"

He wouldn't say no. He told me it was none of my damn business what he did or what he thought, then he looked to Roy and LaFesha and said, "Nothin' personal, you guys. I just like to get under Dupree's skin once in a while." Both Edwards and Severs told him it was nothing to joke about, but O'Brian just shrugged and said, "Hey, Coach, it's my vote."

Boy, one of these days I'd like to get a shot at O'Brian. I know he can catch a baseball coming down the pipe eighty miles an hour; I wonder if he can catch my foot before it gets to his ear at about that speed. Unfortunately, Max won't turn me loose with all these killer moves he's taught me on the karate mat. He told me once, and that was enough, if he ever caught me using them anywhere it wasn't absolutely necessary, he'd never have anything to do with me again. I believe he means it, and that makes O'Brian absolutely safe from my wrath unless he tries to do me in. There have been many occasions when I think it's a crying shame.

I talked to Max the day after the Council meeting, right before his English class—Max is one of those utility teachers who teach in several departments—and unloaded some of my outrage on him. I was secretly hoping he'd be as incensed as I was and free me to kick O'Brian's head off his body, but he just looked up from his desk and said, "Walker, how do you think issues like this get to be important?"

I said I didn't know what he meant.

He said, "The world is full of fools and crackpots—people who were never given any tools to fill their lives up, and who consequently have made their lives so meaningless the only way they can feel good about themselves is to look around and see who they're better than. When they can't find anyone, they create someone. Their ideas are meaningless—right up until we start to fight against them. We're the ones who give power to bigots. We make their ideas real by opposing them."

"Yeah, but, Jeez, Max," I said, "it makes me want to turn O'Brian inside out."

"If you don't learn anything else before you get out of high school," Max said, "learn where to make a stand." He smiled. "Right now make a sit. In your seat. Impossible as the task may seem, it's time for me to make you literate." End of discussion. O'Brian has power only if we give O'Brian power. The gospel according to Max.

You know, it seemed a lot clearer why I was attracted to Devnee when I first started taking her out during the middle of last year. I wonder what happens to true love; where it goes. In the beginning I was always excited about seeing her, and I gave her flowers and candy on special occasions, or on any occasion for that matter, and organized my time around what she wanted to do. But then it started disappearing. Even before I started looking at Elaine as a possible object of my questionable favors, the power of my feelings for Devnee was fading. And I'm such a jerk when that happens. I start creating arguments so she'll get frustrated and mad at me and not want to be around me—in fact, it feels like I'm trying to get her pissed off so she'll break up with me and then I won't have to be the one to do it and feel guilty. It would be one thing if this were the first time, but something close to that has happened *every time*

I've had a girlfriend. It seems really selfish and makes me feel like a lowlife, but it's out of my control. I keep saying I'm going to do it differently, but then I start doing subtle things that I know will irritate them and make them fight with me. They never understand it—which is probably the point—and there's a lot of hurt. And it takes for-frigging-*ever* to finally break up. I hate it. So anyway, even though I'm sure nothing will ever happen between me and Elaine, I'm going to try to break things off with Devnee in a way I can be proud of; you know, take responsibility for letting her know what's going on with me rather than try to make her believe it's her fault, or that some dark, unknown demon is lurking between us. I sure wish I knew why love goes away. Devnee is pretty and she's smart and has a really nice body; small, with a tiny waist and great pecs; dark green eyes and short, almost black hair. She's in the honor society and she plays the piano like a pro. She also likes me a *lot,* which makes it all the harder. Anybody in their right mind is going to say I'm a lunatic for ending it, though there'll be plenty of guys who'll be glad I did. The second I'm gone, her social calendar will be filled up through her first two years of college. And that brings up another thing. Even though I don't want to be with her anymore, *I'm jealous* of anyone else being with her. I can already feel it. God, how do people grow up and get married and live together for the rest of their lives?

December 1

Well, I didn't do such a hot job with Devnee last night. I had it planned to take her out to a nice dinner and find just the right spot to say I didn't want to continue with the relationship. I had a couple of chances, but she looked so nice and so sweet and so full of everything a guy should want in a girlfriend, I started questioning whether I should stick with it. Actually, what really stopped me was I was scared. So another time, I guess. I'll look into hypnosis.

Something more important is pressing and I don't have any idea what to do about it. It's Nortie, and I think it's serious. I mentioned before that he spends time working over at the East Side Childcare Center a couple of nights a week and all day Saturday, unless we work out. He works with the older kids, the first- and second-graders who come after school and on weekends when their parents are working. They're a tough bunch; it's a public-funded daycare and most of the kids are from low- or no-income families; but Nortie does a great job with them. It's the one thing he's really proud of—way more than his swimming. He even invited me over once to watch him work and I have to admit I was amazed. I stayed three hours watching him do science experiments with them, play board games, work on school skills and play outside. He gets them *so* jacked up about learning and discovery, mostly because every time one of them figures out a problem or moves to a higher level in something, Nortie's more excited than the kid. He teaches like he works out—with reckless abandon. If one attack skill doesn't work, he chucks it and goes on to something else. When a kid's having a hard time, he says, "Yeah, that was really hard for me too" and keeps working on it, like it's the most natural thing in the world to have a hard time. Watching him, I was struck by the monumental difference between the way he works with these kids and the way my own daycare and elementary years were. He *never* puts them down. He just doesn't do it, and that's not only with their studies or their quiet time. It's their whole time with him: playtime, lunch, you name it. That doesn't mean he has no discipline; it's that all his discipline is by

41

agreement. He's already gone over with them what is and isn't okay and consequences are already set, so there are rarely hard feelings when Nortie activates them. He gets more respect at the East Side Childcare Center than in all the other places in his life combined. The woman who runs the place—her name's Maybelle Sawyer—says Nortie must have been a big, tough, happy black momma just like her, in his last life.

But this afternoon it all crumbled for him. He's worked himself into a paying position, has several groups of kids that he takes without any supervision, has already decided he's going into elementary education in college—I mean, this is the one thing Nortie is *sure* about in his whole life— and he comes screaming up to my place in his dad's car about 3:00 this afternoon, yelling my name. "Walker! Walker! Oh, God, Walker!" He shot across the lawn and into the house without knocking, and on upstairs, where I was lying on the bed listening to some old pre-Christian Bob Dylan albums that my brother turned me on to. He burst into the room and fell face down on the vacant bed and began sobbing and pounding the pillow. "I'm done! It's all over!" he said again and again, then began convulsing and sobbing even more into the bed. I locked the door, then sat on the bed beside him and put my hand on his back between his shoulder blades. "Nortie," I said, "what are you talking about? What's wrong?"

"I did it!" he sobbed. "I blew it! I blew everything! Oh, God!"

I said, "Nortie, damn it, *what happened?* It can't be this bad."

"It is! It is!" and he sobbed some more.

I let him go for maybe a minute, then rolled him over and grabbed his shoulders. He flinched. "Tell me what happened," I said. "Just tell me what happened."

"I hit a kid, Walk. I hit a little kid. Right on the side of the head."

"On purpose?"

"No," he said. "I mean, yes. I mean, I didn't mean to; I didn't want to. . . . I got *mad.*" The sobbing started again.

I felt the wind go out of me. I don't know much about modern child-rearing practices, but I know physical punishment is *out.* I said, "Nortie, just tell me what happened."

My mom knocked at the door and asked if everything was all right, and I said yeah, everything was fine, that I'd talk to her later.

Nortie sat up and leaned against the wall. "There's this kid named Jamie Crawford; his dad's a local neighborhood drunk, so Jamie's at the Center all the time. Anyway, he came in all pissed off because of something that happened with this girl named Kathy Scarpelli. I don't know what it was because I wasn't out there with them and neither one would tell me. Anyway, we were getting ready to do a science experiment and Jamie wouldn't participate; he just sat over at his desk and pouted. He's a real temperamental kid anyway. I tried to talk him out of it, but he just got madder and madder and I decided to let him work it out for himself. So I was over setting up this experiment with Kathy's group and he started calling her names; really dirty ones. I was the only worker in the room and I was just getting ready to put him away from the group in the Time Out room when he started calling me names too."

He took a deep breath. "I didn't get mad, Walk. Really I didn't. I just ordered him to the Time Out room, and when he wouldn't go, I went over to move him. We do that all the time. He said I was a little faggot and I couldn't tell him what to do. I started to take his arm and move him, and he broke away and ran over and hit Kathy in the middle of the back as hard as he could and called her 'dirty nigger,' then just swept his arm across the table and the experiment went crashing to the floor. I got there and she was screaming and I turned him around to pull him away and he spit in my face." Nortie's face dropped and the tears started coming again. "I slapped him three or four times on the side of the face, Walk. Before I even knew what I was doing. I'm just like my dad." He broke down.

"Nortie," I said, "it can't be as bad as you think. Did any of the other workers come back? Did you talk to anyone?"

He shook his head. "I just ran," he said. "I saw what I did and I ran to the car and came here." He looked to the window, tears still streaming. "I hate my dad, Walk. I thought I loved him, but I hate his guts. I'm just like him."

"You're not like your dad, Nortie. You lost your temper. I'd have thrown the little turd across the room."

He shook his head and grimaced. "I'm supposed to be like a teacher there, Walk. Those are little kids. It's my job to show them the difference. They don't know it, man. I have to show them."

"Look," I said, "let's go talk to Maybelle. I can't believe this can't be fixed. You've put in too much time and work. Let's go back over and see her."

He shook his head. "I can't. I can't go back there now. I couldn't look those kids in the eye. Or Maybelle either. They trusted me."

"Nortie, you've got to. You can't just run away from something like this."

"It's not just them," he said. "It's me. I can't be working with kids if I hit them. Even if they'd let me. I can't do that."

"Nortie, damn it, you don't hit kids. That was a freak thing. You *learned* from it. You're not going to do it again."

He shook his head. "It's just like my dad. Damn it, it's just like all the books say."

I started to stop him, but he held up his hand and told me to just listen for a minute. "You know why I was so good at the Center?"

I shrugged. "You're just good, that's all."

"Nope. When everyone started saying that, I let them think it was true, because it felt so good to have everyone believe I was just naturally good at something. But I read books. *Man,* I read books. When I took Child Development at school, I was the only boy in the class, but I hung right in there. You know why? Because I know if you're abused as a kid there's a good chance you'll grow up and beat on your family. And I'm an abused kid. Boy, you don't know the half of it. My old man's been beating on me as long as I can remember. That day you saw him out in the driveway? Remember? That was like a prelim to what he usually does. Did you know I had an older brother who killed himself before we moved here? He was thirteen years old and he killed himself." Nortie was running full tilt. Tears streamed down his face and snot ran out of his nose and he unloaded. "Thirteen years old and he *killed* himself. He hung himself in our garage. He took a rope and hung himself. Because he was tired of feeling like hell. He was tired of feeling just like I feel around my dad all the time. And you know what else? I'm classic. You could write a book about me. I still *love* my dad. I still try to please him. I can't please him. He doesn't want to be pleased. He wants to be mad. He wants to hate me. He hates me and I just keep going back." Nortie's hands were out, palms up; he was asking for help—from anywhere. "When I hit Jamie, it felt good. I wanted to hurt him. I could feel exactly why my dad hits me."

His last words trailed off a little, like he was running

down. "Look, Nortie," I said finally, "that's what temper feels like. It feels good to everyone to blow up sometimes. That doesn't mean you're like your dad. It means you're like everyone else in the world." I got my coat out of the closet. "Now listen. You stay here. Lock the door and just stay here. I'll make sure no one bothers you; even my parents. Just lock yourself in and stay put. I'll go down and see what the damages are, okay? Just wait here. Somebody needs to tell Maybelle where you are. We'll figure something out."

He started to protest, but I said, "Just promise you'll stay here, okay? You won't have to do anything you don't want to do."

He sank back on the bed and I took his silence as agreement. On the way out, I stopped and asked Mom to please just leave Nortie alone—he was upset, but he was okay. She absent-mindedly said fine and went back to work on her cutwork pillowcases. Then I phoned Elaine and asked if she'd come up and sit down the block in her car and make sure Nortie didn't leave, because it was not lost on me what he'd said about his brother. And no, I *didn't* know he had a brother who killed himself. None of us did.

I hopped in my car and headed for the east side, wondering what I was going to say to whichever childcare worker had walked back into the activity room to find her co-worker gone, two kids wounded and one finely organized science experiment shattered on the floor. Maybe Stotan Week had come early.

The room didn't look as bad as I had imagined. The experiment—whatever it was—was cleaned up and Maybelle had things back under complete control. Jamie the Spitter sat in one corner stretched out in a metal chair, arms folded, staring at his shoes. One side of his face was red and it looked like he might have a mark for a few days. Kathy Scarpelli, whoever she was, was sufficiently recovered to be integrated back into the group and wasn't visibly identifiable. I knew from Nortie's story that she was black, but the group is about a fifty-fifty mix.

I stood in the door and motioned to Maybelle to come over. She was moving about the room as if nothing had happened. When she saw me at the door, she smiled politely and said, "Yes, can I help you?"

I asked if I could talk with her a second.

"Sure, honey," she said, "just a minute." She turned back to the group. "I'm going to be right outside the door for a few minutes. Go on with what you're doing, and if you have a problem, just wait or go on to something else until I get back." She looked at Jamie. "The door will be open, so don't get anything started."

Jamie jammed his chin further into his chest and glared a hole in his shoes.

I identified myself as a friend of Nortie's and she remembered me from the time I came down to watch him.

"Where is he?" she asked.

"He's at my place. He thinks he just jettisoned his career as a molder of young minds."

She looked concerned. "I wish he'd stayed. Running was the worst thing. He left my babies alone." Her eyes went to the ceiling. "Poor Nortie, he must feel a fool."

"At best," I said. "He thinks he's a child-abuser."

Maybelle passed that off. "We're gonna have some trouble with Mr. Crawford," she said. "He can be a bad, bad man when he gets a little drink in him. An' usually what he gets is a *lot* of drink in him. He'll come over here all righteous and nasty, talkin' about how nobody can touch his kid but him. Then he'll take Jamie home and beat hell out of him." She shook her head. "Ain't it a world."

"Should introduce him to Nortie's dad," I said. "They could compare war stories."

"Listen, honey," she said. "You get Norton back over here. I don't know exactly how we can repair this, but I know we can't do it with him hid out in your bedroom. You get him over here, hear?"

I said I'd do my best and thanked her. What a feeling that woman has about her. What a big, powerful, wonderful woman.

When I got back, I saw Elaine's car parked down the block, so I stopped and told her I'd bring her up to date as soon as I checked on Nortie. She was worried, but willing to wait when I said I thought it would be best if she didn't come in just yet. When I got up to my room, though, Nortie was gone; he must have left before she got there. A note on my pillow said: "Thanks, Walk. I've got it back together and I know what I have to do." My heart stopped until I read on: "Don't worry. I'm not my brother. And please don't tell anyone else about him."

I was a little worried because I figured what he "had to do" would more than likely be self-destructive, given his condition at last sight; but I did trust the little maniac not to off himself. There was no way to guess where he'd gone, so I went out and invited Elaine in to bring her up to date and give her a cup of hot chocolate.

CHAPTER 6

December 16
The Eve of Stotan Week

Nortie quit his job over at the East Side Childcare Center. I probably passed him on my way back to my place. He never did see Maybelle face to face or she might have been able to talk him out of it; he just left a note stuck between the door jamb and the knob that said there was no room in that business for guys who lose it. He even sent his last check back—told them to keep it and buy something for the Center. As far as Nortie is concerned, his days of helping kids find their other mitten and ordering *Weekly Reader* are over before they started. That breaks my heart; Nortie will be lost without it. And I don't know what he's going to do about Milika—that's his girlfriend. She works over there too, and he hasn't seen her since the day he quit. She doesn't go to Frost, so he doesn't run into her at school, and even though she's called, she can't seem to get hold of him. She called me a couple of times, trying to locate him, but when I give him the message, he just nods. I think he's too embarrassed. If he doesn't do something about it pretty soon, I'm going to kidnap his young butt and drag him over to see her. He really seems to like her a lot and it must be tearing him up to stay away. That's the dangerous part of Nortie: he keeps everything in and lets it eat out his insides. His relationship with Milika is one that has a strike or two against it from the get-go anyway. Milika's black, and Nortie's dad is hardly a Freedom Rider. I have a feeling if he ever found out, he'd be cutting eye holes in his bedsheets and going out late at night. Milika's dad has the same enlightened views, only in reverse, so Milika would be in the same deep, murky, brown sludge as Nortie if he found out. You talk about clandestine: Nortie and Milika have gone on dates to some of the most obscure places in the Northwest, just to keep anyone from seeing them and telling either of their dads. Sometimes you have to wonder who are the kids and who are the adults. Anyway, I'd hate to see this incident at the daycare mess up their relationship, so if Nortie doesn't do something about it soon, the Great White Captain will have to intervene.

None of us had much trouble talking our parents into letting us spend Stotan Week at Lion's, since it doesn't really affect the Christmas holiday itself. Nortie was really the only one in question, just because his dad is so unpredictable; sometimes he won't let him do things so he can show he has the power, and sometimes he acts like he just doesn't care. Actually, it was harder to get Nortie to come around than it was his dad. He has this illusion that he needs to be around to protect his mother from his dad, and he gets real nervous when he's away for very long. "He just doesn't beat on her as much when I'm around," Nortie said.

"I know, Nortie," I said. "He beats on *you.*"

Nortie nodded and said he guessed that was right.

"Jesus, Nortie, you're the family decoy. You get beat up because your mom won't just get up and leave him. That's not fair."

"Fair" had never occurred to him. "It's not that easy," he said. "It's not that easy to just walk out on somebody you've been married to for twenty-five years."

He was starting to sound defensive and I was feeling myself getting ready to preach, so I backed off. "You're right," I said. "It's probably not that easy."

Anyway, I was able to talk him into coming to Lion's for Stotan Week, which, by the way, is upon us. We borrowed Elaine's dad's pickup last Friday and loaded up some mattresses to keep us off the hard floor and to separate us, by at least a few inches, from the exotic plant and animal life that I'm sure is evolving there. Over the weekend we've been pretty cocky about how much of Max's stuff we can take, but I notice things are fairly quiet around here tonight. We're just lying around waiting for D-Day. We're making it look good, though. Jeff is reading up on world events like he doesn't have a care in the world. He's got a *Time* and a *Newsweek* and a *U.S. News & World Report* and something called the *Christian Science Monitor*. He'll read an article in one, then dig through the others to find which ones carry a report on that same event. He reads them all, then gives us the *Hawkins' Digest* version. Lion, on the other hand, is making no bones about being totally focused on Stotan Week, which is why he's lying on his bed hyperventilating. He wants to go in *ready*. With any luck, he'll pass out from too much oxygen and stop that awful noise for a while. He sounds like a pile-driver.

Nortie's looking a little grim—probably knows that when his dad finds out about what happened at the daycare cen-

51

ter, he'll consider it an offense punishable by much physical violence—so I'm keeping him close. I did notice just after we got here he had to go to the can and a couple of seconds after he closed the door I heard the seat belt click, so he's regaining his sense of humor to some degree. That's certainly preferable to the first few days after he quit the daycare—and got a call from Jamie Crawford's dad. Boy, Old Man Crawford raked him over the coals; even threatened a lawsuit. I figure there ought to be a class-action countersuit on behalf of the world against the Crawfords for letting that little turd live three hours past birth.

Elaine and a couple of her friends plan to come over on Tuesday to make us a decent meal, should we live past Monday. Meanwhile we'll be eating what Jeff assures us is Nature's Perfect Food—peanut-butter and scrambled-egg sandwiches on toasted bread. He swears they're better than they sound.

They sound like hell.

We do have some sense of what Stotan Week will be like because we've been through a few of Max's "Zen" workouts—where everybody gets going so fast and hard that the workout takes on a life of its own. Some of those workouts have gone an hour or more past quitting time, but we were riding so high—and hurting so bad—we didn't even notice. I doubt any of these days will be as easy as the toughest of those. As Max said, he has something he wants us to prove to ourselves. I won't be proving anything if I don't quit thinking about it and get some shut-eye.

MONDAY EVENING

Oh, Lordy, Lordy, Lordy, save me! If I could lift my arms, I'd take up a collection for an automatic weapon and hunt Herb Elliot down like a dirty dog. Max blew even Lion away today. Lion's back over on his bed staring at the ceiling, hyperventilating, but for a different reason. He's trying to get enough oxygen back into his body to get up and go to the bathroom. He'll need the seat belt now just to hold him on.

Max is playing this straight out of *Bridge over the River Kwai*. He showed up with his old Airborne cap and a battery-powered megaphone, lined us up in front of the bulletin board at 8:00 straight up and laid out the rules, which were fairly simple. "Gentlemen," he said. "As I'm sure you know by now, a Stotan is a cross between a Stoic and a Spartan. He's tough and he shows no pain. Directly in front of you, on the board, you see a contract. Step forward, one at a time, and read it. Sign if you still want to participate; don't if you want out. There's still time."

I was at the front end of the line, so I stepped forward and read:

I hereby relinquish ownership of my mind and my body to Max II Song for the days of December 17 through December 21, 1984, all inclusive (hereafter known as Stotan Week) between the hours of 8:00 a.m. and High Noon. During that time I will perform all feats required of me to the *best* of my ability with no visible display of my agony.

I understand that should my mind and/or body fail me and break down, I hold no person or institution responsible, save myself; and should I fail to succeed, fully expect to be washed up into the scum gutter of the Robert Frost High School swimming pool.

Pretty clever, that Max. I smiled and signed, then stepped back and dropped immediately for twenty-five pushups, smiling being a less than Stotanic response. At fifteen I heard Nortie whimper, meaning he had come either to the word "agony" or the part about being washed up into the scum gutter. Nortie joined me.

After we'd all signed, Max laid out the rest: five minutes rest each hour, when the siren went off. He'd brought a goddam hand-crank siren, which he would crank up on the hour; we would stop on the spot for five minutes. Except for those five minutes each hour, our time would be spent in perpetual motion. It was important that we concentrate every minute. Wasted time would be dealt with appropriately. Stotan Week was to be a kaleidoscope of land and water drills, performed so intensely we would transcend our presently accepted limits of emotional stress and physical pain. "When you're starting on the fifteenth lap of a five-hundred-yard freestyle and the guy in the next lane has been on your shoulder all the way, you'll know how deep your well is."

And slowly the kaleidoscope began to turn.

We started with four trips around the deck—a hundred yards per lap—of bearwalk: hands and feet. The pool is an old gray 25-by-25-yard Army Surplus hole in the ground with a rough, spackled deck to prevent slipping. The roughness shredded our hands during the first couple of laps. They won't begin to heal before Friday. Any time Max thought one of us was dogging it in any way, we all stopped the bearwalk on the spot and racked off ten pushups, Max right there with the bullhorn: "What's the matter, Stotan? Quitting so soon?" It's hard to tell which is worse, the stabbing pain in your hands, the ache in your shoulders or Max's taunting in your ear.

From that we went right to the deck drills—jumping in place, pushups, situps, chins on the high-board frame, dips on the low-board frame, switching from one to the other on the whistle, no rest.

"No time for a shower," Max said through the bullhorn,

"but I can't allow your sweaty, slimy bodies in my clean pool," so we stood at attention, turning quarter-turns on the command "Turn, Stotan!" while he hosed us down with the fire hose. "Warm up with an easy four-hundred butterfly," Max said, "and we'll get this show on the road."

There is no such thing as an easy 400-yard butterfly. There's an easy 400-yard freestyle, or breaststroke, or backstroke, but anything over 100 yards of 'fly, at any speed, deserves Dante's serious consideration.

"You'll notice I have one lane roped off," Max said as we finished the 'fly. "For lack of creativity on my part, I'm calling it the Torture Lane. At any point I feel the workout is falling apart or certain of you aren't putting out, we'll go to the Torture Lane. Once there, you will dive in, sprint twenty-five yards, get out and rack off ten pushups, dive back in and repeat—until I stop you. The better job you do during the workout, the fewer times we'll use it." He smiled. "Right now I'd like to see if it works. Line up!"

We lined up single file in front of the Torture Lane and Max blew the whistle, starting us at three-second intervals. We sprinted down one side in single file, got out and racked off the ten, then sprinted back on the other side. Ten push-ups isn't many, but after ten or fifteen full cycles it's all you can do to get out of the water, much less push your body up off the concrete. But Max was there with the bullhorn to help and somehow we got through it.

Then we lined up across the deck for the regular work-out, beginning with thirty 100-yard sprints with time standards, starting every minute and forty-five seconds. For the rest of the day we did sets of 200s, steamrollers (one hard, one easy; two hard, one easy; three hard, one easy; up to ten and back), sprints, two trips to the Torture Lane, then wrapped it up with four more laps bearwalk.

In the shower at a minute past noon we lay on the floor

with all the nozzles turned on hot, oblivious to the plethora of fungi occupying that very same space.

"There was a time there, right before eleven, and then about ten to noon, when we started to fly," Lion said.

Nortie looked over at him like he was crazy. Jeff cranked up a big middle finger. I closed my eyes.

Actually, Lion was right. There were a couple of times when it was so tough it just didn't matter, but most of the time I was aware of trying to save a fraction of myself for the next set. According to Lion, you have to get that out of your head or you'll never fly. Christ! If the good Lord wanted us to fly, he'd have given us hang gliders.

Somehow we pulled ourselves together and made it out through the snow to Lion's Jeepster in the parking lot and piled in. The Jeepster has no top and the temperature outside stood at about twenty degrees, but there was no sense of cold as Lion pulled out of the lot and wound his way through the unplowed neighborhood streets and down to Safeway, where we attempted to buy all the Coke they had in stock and all they ever will have. The first eight bottles were empty before we got them into the Jeepster; we left some fluids back there in that hellhole.

As we lie here on our mattresses, letting KZUU, "The Rock of the Inland Empire," hammer its way into the consciousness of Stotan Week, I ponder a few other constants of this time. One is Jeff's miracle sandwiches. They aren't bad! They're quick, and Jeff makes them for everyone— claims you have to have just the right amount of each ingredient—so no one has to cook. That's a plus. And there's Nortie's St. Christopher medal, speaking of constants. It counts every pushup we do. ("You Stotans think that's funny? Drop for ten!" chink . . . chink . . . chink . . . "You're dogging it, give me ten!" chink . . . chink . . .

chink . . .) If I can get my hands on him, St. Christopher's going on a trip.

We canceled all our pressing social engagements for this afternoon and evening in favor of lying in our sleeping bags listening to rock and roll, reading and otherwise burning not one calorie more than is absolutely necessary. The fatigue in my body goes to the marrow. My guess is that tomorrow morning that fatigue will be replaced by something very close to excruciating pain.

TUESDAY

I was right. I woke up this morning pinned to the mattress with deep-burning muscle pain. My *spleen* was sore. My *liver* was sore. Nothing worked like it was supposed to; I felt like a stumbling toddler learning to move all over again.

From the time the alarm went off until we arrived at the pool, not a complete sentence was uttered—unless the Lord's name in vain can be considered a complete sentence, and I think it's missing a verb. The heater wasn't working and it had to be forty degrees in the room; sitting on the freezing toilet seat was our first Stotan surprise of the day.

We grabbed our suits and towels, pulled on our coats and gloves and boots like grumpy little kids being forced out into the snow to play, and piled back into Lion's Jeepster. I have to say one of the worst parts of the whole day was driving through the neighborhoods toward the pool, anticipating four more hours as a wus posing as a Stotan. I couldn't imagine it being over. When I was a little kid and had to go to the dentist, the only way I could get through the "death walk," where you're riding up in the elevator, then walking down the hall to his office, hearing imaginary screams, was to think about how in an hour or so it would be over. No matter how bad it got, how many live nerves he accidentally drilled, I'd walk out of there alive in about an hour. Well, I couldn't even see an hour into this day, much less clear through to noon. It seemed as if we were headed into something dark and ugly from which there was no return. We were getting on the MTA (one of Long John's old favorites).

After forty-five minutes of non-stop land drills and a good hosing off by Fireman Max, Lion showed his first signs of cracking. We were lined up ready for the 400-'fly warmup when Lion suddenly did a perfect military about-face, a left-face, marched to the low board, up and out to the end, did another perfect about-face, folded his arms over his stomach and fell straight backward into the pool, his back slapping the water like a wet carp on a flat rock. As he fell, he screamed, "Stotan!" We stared a split second in stunned amazement as he started his 400 'fly, before Nortie and Jeff and I followed suit, dropping off the end of the board like ducks in an arcade, then fishtailing off to our lanes to complete the warmup. Peckerhead Lion wasn't going to get ahead of *us* on pain.

Again the whirlwind of non-stop land and water drills; sets of 400s, bearwalk, steamrollers, deck drills, four *long* trips to the Torture Lane, situps on raw tailbones, sets of no-breathe springs, Max hollering all the way, "You have to let go! Give it up! You can't beat it! You're in it! You're part of it! Give it up!"

Lion was the first to slip in. Suddenly he was swimming faster than all of us, getting half again as many repetitions on any given drill, his chest bouncing off the deck in accelerating cadence as he racked off an infinity of pushups. Then Jeff, in less maniacal fashion, started picking up until he was in perfect rhythm with Lion. I looked at Nortie struggling to get himself out of the water and said, "Let's get it, young feller."

Somewhere in the next couple of repeats I noticed things going soft at the edges; and we were a machine. Max put the bullhorn down and just called the starts. He didn't call out times or shout encouragement, or in any way risk jolting us out of the spell.

And then it was noon; a letdown to stop.

In the shower no one spoke. That kind of high makes "normal" seem abysmal, and we tried to hang on to it as long as we could. I felt almost hung over as the exhaustion and the deep, deep muscle fatigue crept back into my consciousness. The soreness was gone, but it would return—physical pain that comes from the soul rather than from outside.

We picked up our Coke and more eggs at Safeway—which is fast becoming our only connection to the outside world—and went straight back to Lion's. The heater was still on the blink, so we crawled into our bags fully dressed, thinking we could fix it later.

Still no one mentioned what had happened—how the workout had just taken over—define it and it goes away—but I'm sure we all hoped we could re-create it tomorrow; we dreaded the idea of going through *half* that in a conscious state.

We passed up the gourmet sandwiches for sleep—drifting off into that totally relaxed, dreamless sleep your body goes to, looking for the state nearest death.

I woke up in the late-afternoon dimness—maybe around four—to scuffling coming from Lion's bed. Jeff was on top of him, pinning Lion's arms to his mattress with his knees. Jeff hollered for Nortie, who came flying up out of his sleep to the bed before he even knew why he was there.

"Beat on his chest!" Jeff said.

"Beat on my chest and die!" was Lion's reply.

"Don't beat on his chest and die!" Jeff said.

Nortie looked to me. "Flip a coin," I said. "You're going to die."

"Why am I beating on his chest?" Nortie asked.

"Just do it!"

Nortie started pounding on Lion's chest with his middle knuckle, like Jeff does to Nortie all the time.

"Why is he pounding on my chest?" Lion asked.

"Because my back hurts," Jeff said. "Because, for a reason I would be far too embarrassed to explain, I fell backward off the diving board today and almost laid my back open so I could keep up some kind of 'Stotan status' with my brain-damaged teammate."

"Yeah," Nortie said, and pounded harder.

Lion let loose with a maniacal laugh, and Nortie quickened the cadence. "Stotan!" Lion screamed. "Stotan! Stotan! All the way! Beat me!" He laughed again.

Jeff pushed Nortie away and pulled Lion's bag up around his shoulders, zipping it up in the same motion. Lion didn't even struggle, just kept up his chant. Jeff stuffed his head down into the bag and closed the top with his fist, then dragged his prize off the bed, out the door, down the stairs, for Chrissakes, and threw it into the snowbank. All to the muffled chant "Stotan! Stotan! All the way!"

Jeff reappeared in seconds, walked into the kitchen and started throwing large globs of peanut butter onto the bread he'd laid out earlier for sandwiches.

I crawled out of my bag and fiddled with the heater for a few seconds, pulling and pushing the frayed cord, and it magically came on. Nortie let out a quick "All right!" and scrambled over to stand by it. "Gotta get warm," he said. "When Lion gets back up here, he's going to beat me to death, and I want to feel it."

Lion stepped back through the door, dragging his snowy sleeping bag, dropped it on the floor, pounded his chest three times and said, "Stotan." He flipped a snowball to Jeff, who dropped it in the sink.

Nortie watched him warily a few seconds to be sure Lion wasn't going to turn on him, breathed an almost inaudible sigh of relief and said, "Boy, we really got hummin' today, huh?"

I said, "Huh."

"How does he do that?" Nortie asked.

"He doesn't do it," Lion said. *"We do it."*

"Yeah," Nortie said, "but I couldn't do it by myself. And I *wouldn't,* either. I mean, it's crazy. You guys know that, don't you? There'll come a time when we ask ourselves why we did it. Like right now. Why are we doing this? Are we jerks?"

"You are," Jeff said, "but that has nothing to do with Stotan Week. Let me give you a little advice. Forget that question until we're out of here. You're either going to do it or you're not. Questions like 'why' only make it tougher."

Nortie grunted in agreement. "What time's Elaine coming anyway?"

"About seven," Jeff said, and came through the kitchen door with the first plateload of sandwiches. "Eat up. Gotta have these gone before she gets here to make us a real meal."

At the sight of the sandwiches, my mouth watered uncontrollably. Christ, even my salivary glands were sore.

It was quiet for the first few minutes we ate, except for a noise that sounded suspiciously like feeding time at the county fair. Then Nortie said, "I wonder if this could hurt us. I mean, I wonder if Max could work us so hard we'd drop dead or something. We get working so hard it doesn't hurt anymore. I mean, it hurts, but I don't care—I just keep swimming harder. Isn't pain supposed to be a signal? I wonder if this is dangerous."

"It's what I've been talking about all the time," Lion said. "It's your mind that stops you from working out like that all the time—protecting you, holding you back. When you let go of the idea that you can't do it, there's nothing to stop you." He rolled over with great difficulty and looked up at the ceiling. "Sometimes when I'm working on a painting—a good one—I'll get going and I can't stop. I see exactly what needs to be where. I'm zipping along miles ahead of what I actually have on the canvas, and the idea of stopping isn't thinkable. I'm into it so much my brain can't tell me it's too good for me to be doing. I've completely lost whole afternoons and nights to that. I think this is how you get *really* good at something."

Nortie nodded and was quiet for a few seconds. Then he said, "Yeah, but these are our *bodies*. How much can they take?"

Jeff looked up from his second sandwich and said, "Want me to tell you how much they can take?"

I said, "Yeah, Dad, tell us a how-much-they-can-take story."

Jeff ignored me.

"Is this a Marine Corps story, Dad?" Lion goaded.

At the end of his junior year, Jeff had an opportunity to sail around the world with a friend of his dad's. The opportunity came after Jeff punched out a student teacher for putting some major moves on his girlfriend, Colleen, and then calling her a tease because she wouldn't respond.

Colleen tried to handle it herself, but couldn't get the guy to back off. So Jeff went into his room with Colleen one night after school and they asked him together to lighten up. He said he would, but things just got worse. Jeff called him down in a Chemistry class one day, and when the guy told him to "grow up," Jeff mopped the place up with him. It might have ended there, but Jeff threatened to light the guy with a Bunsen burner and somebody went for the principal, who at the time was a real hard-ass named Petrie. To make a long story short, Petrie expelled Jeff and told him he would never graduate from Frost—that he was a disgrace and a troublemaker. Jeff probably could have enrolled someplace else—I mean, by law they have to give you an education—but the opportunity for the trip came up and he and his parents jumped on it, figuring he could sit out a year while Petrie lost some of his fervor. To make an even longer story even shorter, they shipwrecked off the Virgin Islands and Jeff was back by Christmas—too soon for Petrie to have cooled off. So, mostly on a whim, Jeff lied about his age and joined the Marine Reserves, figuring he could get the tough part out of the way in the six months between then and summer, then have an obligation for just one weekend a month and a short stint each summer. That way, he figured, with the draft reinstated and prospects of the U.S. sending the cream of its manhood off to collect bullets in some Central or South American country looming, he'd have a better chance to stay away from unfriendly fire. Reserve units go last. He pulled it off as planned and started with us the next year when Petrie was nothing but a miserable memory and Mrs. Stevens was The Man.

"This is a Marine Corps story, son," Jeff said. "Listen up." He settled back with a sandwich, his audience captive in every way.

"When I got to boot camp, I was as cocky as they come. I knew some of these guys were tough, but they didn't have a lifetime of Max in their history. I was in great shape and actually bigger and stronger than most of the guys there; and gung ho? Yes, boys and girls, your redheaded hero was *ready*.

"Well, I really aired it out, taking everything they could hand out and jumping to attention for more, and some of the guys started looking up to me, because I was beating The Man at his own game. Three or four days into it I was *tough*.

"Then one night the sergeant came into the barracks after lights out to rag on us. He did a little impromptu inspection, and those who didn't pass, which was everyone, did pushups and listened to a raft of his crap. Then he moved right up in front of me, which was the reason he was there in the first place, and said, 'Well, Mr. Hawkins. I guess you think you're pretty hot stuff around here,' and I said, 'No, sir. I don't, sir.' He said, 'Don't call me *sir*, you little pimp! I'm a sergeant and you will address me that way!' So I said, 'Yes, Sergeant!' and he said, 'Mr. Hawkins, I want the rest of these men to see you for what you really are. A sister. A warm, wet sister.' I didn't know what to say, so I stood there in my shorts at attention."

"Jeez," Nortie said, "were you scared?" It's hard for Nortie to imagine Jeff afraid of anything.

"Scared drizzly," Jeff said, "but I was still cocky enough not to show it. Sarge pulled his bayonet out of a scabbard stuck in his belt and for a quick second I thought my number was up, but he balanced it on its handle against the wall, blade straight up, and ordered me to come over, lean my back and butt against the wall and slide down to a sitting position just above the blade—like sitting erect in a chair, only there's no chair."

"That sounds hard," Nortie said.

Jeff's eyes rolled. "Not for the first thirty seconds," he said, "but Sarge gave a little speech on courage to the troops standing there by their bunks, put his face down close to mine and said, 'I'll be back, young lady. You better be right there where you are or I'll make the rest of your stay here so miserable you'll wish you'd gone ahead and sat on it,' and he left.

"Well, the sweat ran down my chest and the insides of my arms and my thighs burned and every once in a while I'd feel myself slip a little and I'd push back up. Once I felt the tip of the blade, but Sarge didn't come back. My knees started to shake, but I held on—still acting tough—and guys were whispering to hang in there.

"I heard the door and saw the sarge coming slowly down the hall. He walked up in front of me and said, 'You're a *little* tougher than I thought,' and walked out again."

Even Lion was up on his elbows listening, though I'm sure he'd heard it before.

Jeff started to get up to take a leak, but I yelled, "Finish the story, you jerk!" and he smiled and sat back down on his bag. Jeff has to know he's appreciated.

"Well, then I started to break. Parts of my legs were going numb and I was afraid I couldn't keep control. My butt and lower back were on fire. Tears ran down my face and I started to whimper. Guys were still encouraging me, whispering it would only be a few more seconds, but I broke. I started screaming for Sarge, bawling and wailing and begging. I didn't have the strength left in my legs to push myself up, and the guys were too scared of Sarge to kick the knife out. The door opened and he walked back at his same slow pace. I could feel the point of the blade right there, and I cried and blubbered as he walked toward me. He stood in front of me and kicked the bayonet over, then turned to the troops and said, 'See, I told you he was a sister,' and started to walk out.

"But just as he kicked it out, I checked out. I mean, I

65

checked *out*. He was walking away and I screamed at him: 'Put it back! Get back here, you worthless scum-bag! Put it back!' He whirled around and just stood there, looking at me—and he looked surprised. I screamed, 'Screw you, Sergeant! Put the stinking thing back! What's the matter, *sister?*' I was still in position and I felt like I could hold it forever."

Jeff laughed. "Boy, Sarge didn't know whether to crap his drawers or go blind—he just wasn't programmed for it. So he walked out. I looked at the rest of the guys watching me from their bunks, sort of frozen there, and I held the position maybe thirty more seconds. Then I pushed hard against the wall and stood up."

He looked at Nortie. "Don't worry about your body. It can take a *lot*. Max hasn't tapped anything yet."

Nortie just stared, his mind back somewhere on the pain in Jeff's legs, then snapped to. "That's *your* body," he said. "He's tapped mine." He was quiet a second, then his eyes lit up. "Stotan stories!" he said. "That's what we can do. We can tell Stotan stories. It'll keep us from getting bored. Got any more, Jeff?"

Jeff looked at him, shook his head and turned away.

"It's a good idea," Nortie said, and turned to me. I'd finished my sandwich and was lying on my stomach in my bag, relaxed. "Nortie," I said, "you probably have more Stotan stories than all of us combined. *You* tell a Stotan story."

A thousand hard times must have whipped through his mind, and his face showed a little piece of each one, but he just raised his eyebrows and put his chin in his hands.

"I *do* have a Stotan story, as a matter of fact," Nortie said. It was several hours later and Elaine had sent a friend over to tell us something had come up and she'd have to come tomorrow night. We were getting a little tired of each other's company, so it was disappointing, but we whipped over to Dick's Drive-In and got a six-pack of burgers each to appease ourselves. We were back and about ready to call it a night.

I said, "Let's hear it."

"You've already heard part of it," Nortie said. "Nobody else knows this, so you guys have to promise it doesn't go out of this room, okay?"

"All Stotan stories stay within the brotherhood," Lion said. "New rule."

"It might not be a *real* Stotan story . . ."

"Just tell it, for Chrissakes!" Jeff yelled. "We can give it a title later."

"I used to have a brother," Nortie said, and I knew this was a real Stotan story.

"Really?" Lion said. "I never knew . . ." I raised my hand and shook my head at him. He let it trail off.

"Yeah," Nortie said. "No one around here knows about him. His name was Jeremy. I was six when he died. Exactly six. He died on my birthday."

I said, "Nortie, you don't have to tell this. When I said you must have stories, I meant . . ."

"I need to tell this," he said. "I've had it with me a long time. Is it okay to tell it?"

Lion said, "It's okay to tell it." Lion knows a thing or two about family that used to be.

"My brother was seven years older than me," Nortie said, and smiled. "I was a mistake. A big one, my dad says. Anyway, we lived in a small town called Beaumont in Nebraska and my dad was a truck-driver. He was *really* mean then. He used to do real damage. He drank a lot— way more than now—and he'd come home some nights in a rage. He'd drag everyone out of bed and choose one of us to pick on—usually Mom or Jeremy, because they protected me. He'd call us names and ask why the hell we were trying to ruin him and make wild accusations until either Mom or Jeremy had had enough and challenged him. Then he'd knock them around and storm out. We'd comfort each other and finally go back to bed and Dad would stay away a day or so—or go out on a haul—and then come back like nothing had happened. No one would mention it, but you could see Jeremy starting to hate him. And I didn't understand that then, because Jeremy talked about all the things he wanted to do to Dad, and *would* do as soon as he was big enough; but then I'd see him trying to please him all the damn time. He'd go out and wash his truck—once he even *waxed* it. A whole truck he waxed. It was a monster. And I'd want to ask him why. I wanted to ask him why he did anything nice for Dad. But I didn't ask. And I understand now, because I do it all the time.

"I remember one night Dad came home drunk and decided Mom had been sleeping around, so he called her a whore and a bitch and some names a whole lot worse than those. She stood there crying, asking how he could be so mean when he just knew that wasn't true. But he wouldn't give it up, and he started describing what she did with all these other guys she was messing with. Finally, he made her stand up on this big round coffee table so her kids could get a good look at their mother, the whore. Jeremy cried and held my head against his chest so I couldn't look, and Dad came over and jerked him away and threw him against the kitchen table. Then he made me throw things at Mom. He stood there slapping me on the back of the head until I did it. I said, 'No!' and he'd slap me, and then he started to choke me. Mom was begging me to go ahead, and Jeremy was trying to get up to come help, but his arm was broken. Finally, I threw an ash tray at her, and I think a small vase that was on a TV tray. Neither one hit her, but somehow it satisfied him, and he called us all some more names and left.

"Jeremy was thirteen years old, and I think he thought Dad had finally gone too far; that we'd pack up and leave, because that's what Mom said. But the next morning, when she took us to the hospital to have his arm set and put in a cast, she told the doctor that he'd broken it falling off the garage roof. I remember the look on his face like it was yesterday. I think he hated her more for that than he hated my dad. He knew right then we were stuck with it forever, and he hated himself for not being able to make it better.

"The next day Mom sent me out to the garage to see the bike they got me for my birthday, and to get Jeremy to come in and watch me open the rest of my presents. Dad was on the road.

"The garage was just off the kitchen, and I walked through the door and Jeremy had hung himself from the rafters. A stepladder was kicked over and his Adidas dangled right above my eye level. There was a note tied to one of them with my name on it.

"I was a Stotan, guys. I was tough and I showed no pain, as Max says. I walked over and took the note, turned around and went back into the house and up to my room. I didn't cry or say a word; just crawled under the covers. A couple of weeks later I read the note. All it said was Jeremy was sorry; that I'd have to take care of myself. He wished me good luck."

Nortie told the story without changing tone or expression once. Jeff and I were paralyzed; staring at him, waiting for more; waiting for the rest. Tears streamed down Lion's face and he rolled over and faced the wall.

"I don't even know what happened after that," Nortie said. "I don't know how Mom got him down or how they notified my dad or what happened to the bike. Neither of my parents ever said another word about it—at least not to me. In a few months we moved. I think we moved about four times in the next couple of years until we showed up here. My dad's been at the hardware store ever since. He doesn't drink as much as he used to, and he doesn't beat on us as much."

I finally said, "Nortie, is there anything we can do?"

"Nope," he said. "I just needed to tell somebody." He rolled over and laid his head down. "I've been needing to tell somebody for a long time."

Lion saved the day. We lay for those few minutes, dreading going to sleep on Nortie's story. I couldn't imagine having that incident be part of my life, or living with what it must be like to have Mr. Wheeler as a dad. It made me wonder how Nortie got the day-to-day things done—how he got up and went to school, or took out the garbage, or shoveled the walk.

Lion said, "I have a Stotan story that will put yours to shame, Nortie. And it will diminish yours to the rank of 'amusing anecdote,' Jeff."

Jeff said, "So tell it, Anus Breath."

Any story would do.

Lion reached up and switched off the flashlight above his bed, leaving us with only the glow from the streetlight outside and the reddish flash of the neon bar sign. "Close your eyes," he said. "You'll want to visualize this.

"At fourteen—a frosh—I was not quite the fully bloomed Tom Selleck clone you see before you today. While not the King of adolescent clumsiness and buffoonery, I certainly qualified as a Duke or an Earl. And I had the hots for Melissa Lefebvre."

"You and every guy who draws breath," Jeff said.

"Yeah, but I had it *bad.*"

I said, "This is beginning to sound like Melissa Lefebvre's Stotan story."

"Funny man," Lion said. "The girl was enchanted. She just didn't know it. So shut up and let me tell this.

"You guys remember Melissa. Already a varsity cheerleader, she was Sophomore Class President, Frost High School Carnival Queen and carried a 4.0 grade average, with a reputation so pristine you felt the stabbing, twisting saber of guilt the moment you tried to sneak her into one of your fantasies. More than once she turned me into a one-man Ship of Fools with a smile or a nod that wasn't even meant for me. A curious mixture of tomboy and princess, those subtle dimples, long brown hair and light blue eyes just made you ache."

Jeff let out big air. "This isn't a Stotan story," he said. "This is disgusting."

Lion went on as if Jeff hadn't spoken. "I wanted her. But to have her, to really *have* her; to shroud her in the purple-and-gold letter sweater I had yet to earn; to have my class ring wrapped in adhesive tape coated with fingernail polish so it would fit her delicate finger; to meet daily at Dolly's for a chocolate Coke; well, that would have been what you call your amazing come-from-behind victory."

"That would have been an amazing come-from-*way*-behind victory," Jeff said.

"Whatever," Lion said. "Anyway, a few nights before the Football Frolics dance up at the gym, during which I had promised myself to ask her to dance—maybe even a slow one—I was visited upon by the first of a forest of pimples yet to come. This wasn't an advance man, an insignificant pimple scout sent ahead to determine whether this peach-fuzz frontier could support a whole pimple nation. This was Sitting Bull. This pimple was red and sore and angry and given to harmonic tremors. Friends asked if I were growing another head. Enemies said it must be my date to the dance. This was a big zit.

"I considered flying down to some obscure Central or South American country where it's possible to have an illegal alien growing on your face surgically removed, but decided against it, because I was fortunate in those days to count among my friends one Walker Dupree, a promising young swimmer and budding sports-medicine specialist, ready with a quick remedy for my leprous condition."

I was already laughing—I knew this story. "Really," I said, "it worked for me."

It was as if I hadn't spoken—or didn't exist. "After close examination," he went on, "my friend Walker recommended Coke-bottle treatment. 'I beat it to death with a Coke bottle?' I gasped, then considered it. 'That *might* work.'

"But Walker revealed to me a nearly invisible scar from a boil on his right calf that he had treated with this method just three days earlier.

"That night, with my parents finally tucked away in their beds, I closed myself in the kitchen, quietly boiled a Coke bottle in water and deposited a wet washrag in the freezer. When the water came to a rolling boil and the rag was nearly stiff, I carefully removed the bottle with tongs, wrapped it in the freezing washrag and slipped the piping-hot mouth over the mountainous zit—the idea being that as the air inside cooled and contracted, it would suck the boiling core of the Vesuvian blemish *whappo!* right into the bottle, rendering it dormant and harmless.

"It didn't come off as advertised."

I said, "You must not have done it right."

"As the air inside the bottle contracted," Lion continued, ignoring me, "my forehead drew tighter and tighter;

my eyes bulged. The pimple didn't pop; just extended like a throbbing finger deeper and deeper into the neck of the bottle. *It wasn't working!* I pulled on the bottle to remove it, but it was sucking my face off my head. I thought, 'I'm going to have to wear this bottle to the dance. Melissa won't be impressed.'

"With that horrifying fate in mind, I gripped the bottle in both hands, closed my eyes, gritted my teeth and yanked. It popped free with the sound of two anteaters kissing in an echo chamber.

"Tremendous relief washed over me as I sank to the kitchen floor. Given the alternative, I was more than happy to escort the throbbing postule to the Football Frolics.

"But in the bathroom I gazed into the mirror and changed my mind. The mouth of the bottle had left a deep purple ring around the angry sore, forming a perfect three-dimensional bull's-eye right in the middle of my head.

"At the dance, after an infinity of I'll-ask-her-for-the-next-slow-ones, I screwed up the courage to do just that, and we glided across the dimly lit dance floor beneath the purple-and-gold crepe-paper streamers, two jerky steps forward, one jerky step back, at arm's length.

"Melissa peered deeply into my eyes. 'Is that a corn plaster on your forehead?' she asked romantically.

"I acknowledged that it was. 'I was showing some of the football players how to do a head spear,' I said, 'and drove a loose rivet in the helmet I'd borrowed into my forehead. No big deal.'

"'That must've hurt,' she said, nodding. 'It got you right on that monstrous pimple.'"

CHAPTER 7

We flew through most of the workout today on the Norton Wheeler Express. Nortie was feeling so good about unloading the weight of his brother that he didn't care how badly Max hurt him. We didn't talk much last night, even after Lion lightened things up with his tale of the Pimple That Ate Serbousek, but one thing is sure: Nortie doesn't have to carry that around by himself anymore. I was glad that Elaine and her friends didn't make it over; that whatever magical bond Nortie's tale created among us wasn't broken. Jeff went out into the kitchen to make us another round of sandwiches, and KZUU sang us off to sleep.

When we got up this morning, there was a lot less bitching and moaning and general dread and more a sense of going up there to take on The Man together. Somewhere early in the workout, just after we stood at closed-ranks attention for our post-warmup hosing down, the back of

Lion's suit clutched tightly in Jeff's fist to prevent him from attempting some kind of new and torturous entry into the water, I followed Nortie into that soft-bordered world where my body is capable of doing whatever it will. The other guys fell in and our little machine hummed right through both five-minute breaks. Max had said all along that those five minutes were our time to do with what we pleased, so we spent one of them in the Torture Lane and the other doing no-breath sprints.

I think all swimmers use some kind of gimmick to keep them going during the really tough spots in workouts. I knew a state champ from two years ago who imagined a shark at his toes and got into swimming for his life. Jeff says he uses Colleen, his girlfriend, beckoning him from the far end of the pool in a translucent black negligee. He goes on with that description, but I'll spare you. Who knows what Lion uses? Probably something new and different from his bag of wizards and dragons and sorcerers for each lap he swims. I've tried them all—usually I tell Jeff I use Colleen too, same negligee, same sordid details, just like the football team does on their wind sprints—but today I used Nortie's brother, Jeremy. And so did Nortie. He had told his story and not been condemned to rot in Hell for letting it out, and now, for the first time, it seemed like he might be able to use the power of Jeremy's memory for something positive in his life, rather than just a hammering reminder that the world can turn on you in the wink of an eye, with no warning whatsoever; no thirty-day notice to get your things in order. Because of what he got back from us; because our response to his story was to give him a Stotan Day, a day in which *no one backed off,* I think he got a taste of something that's been absent all his life: trust.

I know Max couldn't have had any idea what was going on, though every once in a while he makes you think that he knows everything by the way he just goes with it. It took him three or four reps of the first set of 200s to realize how things were, and he did his part by keeping the pressure right up there at the edge. After the first ten minutes or so, the bullhorn was nowhere in sight and the Airborne cap mysteriously disappeared. We did fewer deck drills and more swimming, with Max cutting back on the rest intervals between reps, subtly, a few seconds at a time, until we were getting not one second more than we needed and still holding time standards. That's what Max has: touch. He knows when to put on the pressure, how to hold it and when to back off for room. Max Il Song is the Prince of Touch.

The trip back to reality wasn't as rough today. This Stotan stuff seems to be taking hold. After we lay on the shower floor awhile, I glanced up to see Lion looking over at Nortie, who was leaning up against the wall, watching the water hammer on his stomach. He said, "Nortie, you did the right thing, telling us." Nortie looked straight back at him, eyebrows raised, lips pursed, and nodded.

We didn't just go back and hole up all day today like we did for the past two. Some of the soreness and stiffness is starting to recede and we're feeling more like human beings again, so we decided to get out and around a little bit. It was a day without scrambled-egg and peanut-butter sandwiches. First, we hit the Savage House, Spokane's premier pizza place, and fairly astonished their lunchtime crew with the sheer bulk of what we ingested. Savage House management may think twice before choosing to continue their "Wednesday Lunch Special—all you can eat for $2.99." Then we whipped downtown to catch a matinee before heading back to Lion's dungeon to prepare for Elaine and her friends, which is to say straighten out the sleeping bags and make sure the heater was working. Along about six

Jeff and I decided to run over to the drugstore and get some toothpaste and maybe a couple of comic books for distraction. We were thumbing through the somewhat limited selection when I happened to look out the plate-glass window to see O'Brian walking toward the entrance with a bundle under his arm. He dropped the bundle on the sidewalk beside the three newspaper racks standing there and snipped the wire that held it together with wire-cutters. I didn't recognize the guy with him, but he was carrying several identical bundles. They talked for a quick second, then walked off across the parking lot.

Jeff and I paid for our stuff—I told the man behind the counter it might be in his best interest to strip-search Jeff— and we split. Outside, I didn't have to look for more than a second to know the contents of O'Brian's cargo. That unconscious jerk-off is a paper boy for those Aryan Nation idiots over in Falls Lake. The small sign they left beside the papers said it all: TAKE ONE—LEARN THE TRUTH. We picked up one of the papers and walked back across the street to Lion's, deciding not to tell Lion yet because we didn't want to spend the rest of the evening hunting O'Brian down like the scum he is and spreading his body parts over the city.

Shortly after we got back, we heard a car pull up outside, then the sounds of girls' voices. Nortie got up and looked out the window and said, "Uh-oh."

I said, "What?"

"Elaine's here," he said.

"So, what's 'uh-oh' about that?"

"Milika's with her." He rubbed his hands on the front of his pants. "Oh, Jeez," he said, "I haven't seen her since I quit the Center."

"You haven't even called her?" Jeff asked.

Nortie shook his head.

Jeff said, "Uh-oh."

"She's gonna pop you upside the head," Lion said.

"If I'm *lucky*. God, I should have at least called."

"Twenty-twenty vision," I said. "The man's a romantic genius. A modern-day Errol Flynn."

Jeff answered the knock at the door. Nortie looked as if he were visualizing Milika standing on the other side wrapping her fist around a roll of quarters so she could put him away with one punch. The two of them entered laden with grocery sacks; evidently Elaine's other friends couldn't make it. Milika set her groceries on the counter, then turned around and looked at Nortie, who was standing over by Lion's bed with his hands in his pockets. He started to shrug and she marched across the room and whapped him alongside the ear with an open hand.

Jeff looked to Elaine. "You women are so predictable," he said.

"What's the matter with you?" Milika yelled at Nortie.

"I—"

"Where you been? Why didn't you call me? No wonder your dad hits you." She started to take another shot at the side of his head, but he flinched and she held back. "You think you'd just never see me again? You think you can crawl off and disappear?"

"I didn't—"

"You *going* with me or what? You don't treat me like that, understand?"

"I didn't—"

"You understand?"

Nortie nodded. "Yeah, I understand. I'm sorry."

Milika softened a little. "Yeah, well," she said, "sorry don't get it. I got no time to spend with someone who won't talk to me. Don't be sorry, just don't ever do it again, okay?"

Nortie smiled. "Yeah, okay."

Milika started to walk back to the counter, but turned in the middle of the room and looked straight back at Nortie. She said, "Next time I hit you, hit me back. You want to be my man, you don't take that from anybody."

Poor little turd just can't win.

"So what's to eat?" I asked Elaine, hoping to end the ambush.

She reached into one of the bags, dragged out a dozen weiners and said, "We're going to have a weenie roast. I brought sticks and buns and mustard and ketchup, and I have wood in the car. Move over, Annette Funnyjello, we're having a beach party."

"You may not have noticed," I said, "but along with everything else this place doesn't have, it doesn't have a fireplace."

"You don't roast weenies and marshmallows indoors, you silly goose," she said. "We'll roast 'em down in the alley."

"It's fifteen degrees out there," I said.

"That makes it five degrees warmer than it is in here," Milika said, and she was close to right—the heater had been performing less than admirably all day long and it was looking to be the coldest night of the week.

Past experience told us that if you're going to argue with Elaine, you have to *want* to argue, and none of us did, so we had a damn weenie roast. We sat on the hoods of my car and Elaine's, and Lion's Jeepster in the alley behind the Fireside, dressed in every stitch of warm clothes we had; built a fire and stuffed ourselves with hot dogs and marshmallows and, except for the snow and the cold and the unlikely surroundings and the fact that there isn't a body of water within a hundred miles of here that isn't frozen solid, it was a beach party. The fire crackled and sizzled and our shadows danced on the side of the Fireside Tavern and something about the whole stupid experience was a little bit magic—until the fire burned down and something about the whole stupid experience was colder than hell.

We went back inside, Nortie holding back a little with Milika, probably trying his hand at another apology, and stuffed towels in the cracks around the windows and doors and beat on the heater a little—Lion went down into the Fireside to make sure it was plugged in well—and things warmed up a little. We made Elaine insanely jealous with stories of Stotan Week and she lamented the fact that there's no place for women to have the experience we were having. "Sure there is," Nortie said, "when they die and go to Hell."

Milika, on the other hand, was absolutely content with the knowledge that there isn't a place for girls to have the experience we were having.

Around nine o'clock Elaine produced four straws in her hand. "Short straw gets the Elaine Ferral no-mercy, full-body massage, guaranteed to relax every muscle Max has ambushed. The massage will be the product of six weeks of intense training at Gary Takashita's massage school—a blending of styles from the East and West. It is non-sexual in nature, and if the recipient makes one false move, I'll tear his arm off."

I've never won anything in my life, never even a single game of Bingo—hardly a coin-flip—but I drew the short straw, an obvious move on the part of the gods to let Elaine get her hands on me and fall forever in love. When the cries of "Fix!" died away and those reptiles crawled off into their bags, Elaine told me to put on my suit and lie down on the bag. It was chilly, but once she started in, the temperature in my body was the only one that mattered to me.

That massage had to be one of the most wonderful things I've ever felt. She started with my shoulders and neck and worked for at least an hour, working over every muscle Stotan Week had bushwhacked. She used a continuous deep rolling motion that took all the tension down and out through my fingers and toes. She even massaged my face.

We all talked for a while—every once in a while I'd moan and Jeff and Lion would threaten my life—until everyone else had drifted off. By the time she finished, I was convinced she was hopelessly, terminally in love with me and that I should describe in lurid detail every fantastic hallucination I'd had about her in the past few months. She saved me from that by going once quickly over my shoulders again, hard, then slapping my back. "Gotta go," she said. "Make tomorrow a good one." She gently shook Milika awake, and they were gone. Boy, I hate this. One of these days I *have* to check her out. Soon. Soon as I clean things up with Devnee. I'll do that tomorrow.

THURSDAY

The magic was gone today. Oh, God, was the magic gone. You never want to turn your back on something as tough as Stotan Week; take it for granted in any way and it'll sneak up from behind and hit you on the back of the head with a pickax. We did and it did. Today we went up there thinking we had it knocked. Three days down, two to go; all the confidence in the world after humming through yesterday in a magical fog. What we forgot was you have to *do* it, and you have to do it *all out,* and if you don't, it won't work and you will be sorry.

We must have spent half our time today in the Torture Lane. Max used the bullhorn like it was growing out of his face, and he must have thrown the siren into the deep end, because there wasn't even a sniff of a five-minute rest period. And Jeff let Lion off his leash. Christ, we're headed around the pool deck on what must have been our fiftieth lap of bearwalk when, instead of taking a right to continue around the pool, that peckerbrain takes a left and heads for the door. The door to *outside*. It's twenty-two degrees out there, semi-blizzard conditions, we're soaking wet and dog tired and that stark raving brain-damaged lunatic takes us on a bearwalk across the tundra. "Stotan! Stotan! All the way!" he yelled as he butted the door open with his head and forged his way through—*through*, not *over*—the snowbank next to the sidewalk and out to the fence, then across the yard and back through the other door and into the Torture Lane, the three of us following dutifully behind him, swearing we're going to rip his arms and legs from his body and let Marty O'Brian use his torso for a chest-protector.

Actually, the wonder of it all doesn't strike when you plunge into the snow—you have enough body heat going to keep you warm for quite a while out there. And it's less work because you can put your hands out in front of you and sled along, which takes quite a bit of pressure off your shoulders; and certainly the snow is kinder to your hands than the rough deck. No, the wonder of it all becomes apparent when your twenty-two-degree hands hit the seventy-degree water. It felt like I was wringing out a beehive. At the end of the first lap of the Torture Lane, Lion was out of the water, yelling, "Stotan!" at the top of his lungs with each pushup and Jeff dropped with his face inches from Lion's ear. Between Lion's chants, Jeff whispered, "Your stuff is in the street." Lion jumped up, must have dived half the length of the pool, screaming, "All the way!"

Over on the side, Max smiled.

But there was no dragging us into that magic Twilight Zone. I felt every stroke I swam today; every pushup. When it was over, all I could do was drop to the floor of the shower and praise the gods for not stopping time completely.

"Serbousek," Jeff said, "you must be a very old man."

"Why's that?" Lion asked.

"Because you're so close to death. If I cough once, or sneeze, or have the slightest hint of a sniffle, you're as old as you'll ever get."

Lion smiled and sank against the wall. "You won't get sick," he said. "They do that all the time in Norway, or one of those places. Actually, I only did it because it's so good for us."

"Well, it wasn't good for *you*," Jeff said. "Don't sleep. Don't turn your back on me for a second."

Lion's high-pitched giggle bounced around the shower like a rubber bullet.

Bad as it was, there's only one more day of it. We've got it beat. We won't take it for granted again, though: guaranteed.

Lion may have a little tougher time with the last day of Stotan Week than the rest of us, because he did serious bodily damage to himself tonight after we'd devoured the last of the sandwiches and lay basking in the glory of having whipped four fifths of Stotan Week.

"Gather 'round, Stotans," he yelled from the kitchen, where he stood stark raving naked atop the stove, his tank suit in one hand and Max's bullhorn in the other, as Jeff walked through the door with groceries for dinner. Jeff looked impressed; he stood in the doorway, semi-awestruck. I still have no idea how Lion got away from the

83

pool with Max's bullhorn, but there it was, and there he stood.

"Gather 'round, Stotans!" Lion said again, this time through the bullhorn; and the walls rattled. "Having successfully completed four days of Stotan Week, you have earned the sacred privilege of learning the true mystical secret of Stotanism—at least, as it applies to aquatic endeavors."

"Tell us, Master, O ye of the sunken chest," Jeff said, "what is the secret?"

Lion looked down at his chest, then back at Jeff with exaggerated haughty contempt, and continued. "You have been led to believe that the great swimmers of modern times are just like us. 'They put on their suits the same way you do; one leg at a time,' I believe is the way Max puts it. Well, I am here today to tell you that is simply not true. My uncle had the privilege in his youth, lo these many years ago, to swim against one Don Schollander at a Meet of Champions in Portland, Oregon. Uncle Jake happened to be in the locker room, taking a leak, as they say, when Don was suiting up, and witnessed the secret of Don's magic. Yes, my children, Don Schollander was a closet Stotan. My uncle passed that secret down to me and I am here tonight to pass it on to you."

With that, he handed the bullhorn down to me, stretched his suit open with both hands, leaped into the air, doubling both knees to his chest, and attempted to thrust both legs through the leg holes at once. He caught the little toe of his right foot on the suit and fell sideways all the way to the floor, onto his shoulder. Jeff was able to break his fall some, which is the only reason Lion didn't break his arm, but it knocked the wind out of him and I'll be surprised if at least one rib isn't cracked. Somehow in the chaos we got him safely to his bag, clutching his ribs and cursing Don

Schollander. Jeez, the way Stotan Week is going, I'm surprised we didn't all follow suit, like we did off the diving board.

After dinner tonight I called Devnee and went out for a couple of hours, though the rest of the guys said I was exhibiting conduct unbecoming a Stotan by spending even that much time on a "date" with a girl during this holiest of weeks. It wasn't exactly meant to be that. I'd decided part of being a real Stotan was "getting clean." That was how I felt when we came out of the workouts; that's what I thought had happened for Nortie when he told us about his brother killing himself. "Getting clean" translates into "telling the truth" for me as far as Devnee is concerned, so I decided to take her someplace and break off our relationship—tell her the truth, that it just isn't powerful for me anymore. Tell it like it is, Captain.

I picked her up about seven and we drove over to Dick's Drive-In for a Coke. She looked so pretty, so squeaky clean and shiny, that I knew I'd have a *lot* of trouble with this.

"I've missed you," she said as we drove down the arterial from her place toward Dick's. I'd told her I wouldn't be around much during Stotan Week, that I needed to concentrate on workouts. That was okay with her.

"Really?" I said.

She laughed and reached over to kiss me on the neck. "Of course, dummy. What do you think? You miss me?"

My resolve eroded a little. "Sure did," I lied. Truth was, except for feeling pangs of guilt because of my uncontrollable attraction to Elaine, I hadn't even thought about Devnee. "Missed you a lot, though we've been pretty busy—and pretty tired."

She moved over closer and rubbed my neck. Her hands are strong but no match for Elaine's in either strength or touch. I tried pushing comparisons out of my mind. They wouldn't go.

"How are the other guys holding up?" she asked. "Are you all becoming big, tough Stotans who leap tall buildings and eat your young?"

I said, "Looks like it," and told her of Lion's shenanigans, falling off the board and taking us out into the arctic air. I tried not to get comfortable with her so this would be easier, but it wasn't working. Besides going together, Devnee and I are good friends and have been for quite a while. Everything here felt like betrayal of that friendship. Somewhere in the middle of it all, just before I abandoned the idea of pulling this off with any grace—or pulling it off at all—I realized that if I were going to *really* be honest, I would have to tell Devnee about Elaine, even though there isn't really anything to tell in terms of action; and that to do that I would have to tell Elaine too, as well as the rest of the guys. What I ended up with was Scrambled Innards, a condition in which my stomach turns inside out, I abandon all stressful plans and shine it on.

Devnee and I drove out Division Street to Diamond Bowl and bowled a few games. As usual, we had a good time and I talked myself into believing Christmas wasn't the right time to break up with your girlfriend anyway. I took her home by nine, we made out in front of her house for a little while, which further convinced me I hadn't explored all the possibilities of this relationship yet, and she got out.

"Call me tomorrow when you're finished?" she asked.

I said I would.

I'm not much one to share my innermost feelings with the guys, close as we are, so nobody suspects my dilemma. When I got back, they made all the rude comments you'd expect from guys surrounded by civilization, yet remaining untouched by it in any way. I made a motion that we all turn in and get the sleep we'll need for tomorrow. When the lights were out and we lay there watching the corners of the room dance in muted red to the uneven cadence of the neon Fireside sign flashing just outside and below the window, Jeff said, "Hey, Walk. I told Serbousek where we saw O'Brian yesterday."

I said, "So, Lion, what are you doing here? How come you're not sniffing that scum-bag out of his hole?"

"I'm injured," he said. "I'll kill him later."

FRIDAY

We awoke by six this morning—charged up. Lion felt a lot better and was having only a little trouble with deep breaths, so I guess his rib isn't cracked, maybe only bruised. We got to the pool a little early and he put the bullhorn back in the equipment room, but when Max came out on the deck, he didn't have it. The military posture was gone: no captain's hat, no bull. He just walked out on the deck and said, "Guys, today we swim. No bearwalk, no deck drills." He looked directly at Lion. "No romping in the snow. You're swimmers and that's what you're going to do." He didn't talk about how hard we should work or that we'd get out of it only what we put in, or any of that crap. He just started us swimming. Every second repeat was 'fly, and if I've said it once, I'll say it a thousand times, my vision of Hell is swimming butterfly down a one-lane pool toward Eternity.

There wasn't a pushup or situp done, not a dip or a yard of bearwalk; just us plowing through the water. When one of us started to fade, the others were right there helping—pushing, pulling. Nothing was going to keep us from completing Stotan Week in style. Max systematically cut back on the rest between repeats and kept the pressure right at the outer edge, and we turned up the heat.

At about 11:00 Lion jumped out, clutching his rib, and yelled, "To the Torture Lane!" Max let us go for about a half-hour and we did one lap freestyle, ten pushups; one lap 'fly, ten pushups; one lap free . . .

It was mind-boggling. We felt every lap, every pushup, but kept each other going on sheer will. There was nothing mystical or magical about it, just raw physical and mental tenacity.

At 11:30 Max blew the whistle, and we had to hold Lion. Jeff got up on the low board and cannonballed about an inch from his head and the rest of us tied him up. He went limp, and we let go, then he tried to swim away. What a hot dog.

When we got to the edge of the pool, Max said, "Let's call it early. I'm bored with this crap."

We soaked him as he flip-flopped off into his office. When we got out of the shower, Max was nowhere to be found. The pool was locked and the lights in his office were out. We thought we'd missed him, so we headed for the Jeepster, but he was standing beside his car in the parking lot with a paper sack.

"I'm going to say something about this week before you go," he said, and reached down into the sack to fiddle with what was there. "The key is Wednesday, the day you went with it all the way." He played a little more in the sack. "I'm really proud of you guys. You came up with more than even I thought you had. If there really is such a beast as a Stotan, you guys are it—though Stoicism and Spartanism aren't really what it's all about; they're just ways to get there.

"If you think this week was just about swimming, you're missing the part I think is important. If it's only about swimming, you gave up a full week of your lives to shave one, maybe two tenths of a second off times you'll be hitting by the State meet anyway. Heavy payment for so little time."

He put the sack down beside him and looked straight at us. "This week I attempted to take some of the things I learned when I was in Korea and turn them into something useful to you. Remember the times when you gave up the fight and just went with Stotan Week—saw which way the river was flowing and went that way too. Most times the depth of your well isn't measured in how hard you fight—how tough you are—but in your ability to see what is and go with that. If you'd fought me this week, I'd have won."

Then Max's eyes went soft and he folded his arms and leaned against his car. He said, "Guys, it isn't very often in a person's life that he gets to pass on the really important messages, the things he's learned that are sacred to him. And I think it isn't very often he gets to pass them on to exactly the right people. But this is one of those times for me, and I want to thank you for allowing it. There are lessons in this week that can serve you for the rest of your lives—but there aren't words for those lessons, so I can't *tell* you what they are. You find them for yourselves. Just remember, when it's time to meet the Dragon, that you can't fight him head on; he breathes fire. But you can go *with* him and beat him." Max pointed to the sack. "I gotta go," he said. "Got something for you in there." He got into his car and drove away.

I picked up the sack and opened it. Four small boxes, each with one of each of our names on it, lay in the bottom. Each box contained a small gold band with STOTAN lettered across the face and each of our names engraved on the inside. Each was a perfect fit.

CHAPTER 8

January 2

After Stotan Week the vacation went like a flash. They emptied the pool to make some minor repairs, so there were no water workouts, and we had to find other ways to stay in shape. We substituted working out at the local Nautilus and running long distances through the miserable December weather. That, plus the backlog we built up during Stotan Week, left us in pretty good shape to start the season, I think.

After we got our Stotan rings, we drove over to Savage House Pizza to celebrate and talk about what heroes we were. Things seemed in place for all of us. I was settled with my dilemma about Devnee and Elaine, having decided to take the bull by the horns and do nothing; Nortie's mind was a million miles from the daycare center; Lion was as high as I've seen him; and Jeff was even higher, because Colleen was due in from Stanford on a 6:00 flight. We called Elaine to come over and join us and I remember we spent most of the time talking about Max and what a smart motor scooter he must be to have made this work. Elaine is convinced he's a human being of a higher order than the rest of us—that he's here for a reason. That's a part of Elaine I don't understand very well. She believes in former lives and lives to come and karma and that things happen for reasons—that there's a spiritual reality, a cosmic order that exists right under our noses if we'll just look at it. And she thinks Max's soul has been in the universe longer than most. I'm thinking of telling her I believe all those things too so she'll have one more reason to think I'm the budding guru of her dreams, but if I did, I'd be lying. I don't necessarily *not* believe it; it just doesn't affect me much one way or the other. I figure I'm here now, in this body, in this set of circumstances, and I've got my hands full dealing with things I can see and touch and smell and feel. I have to admit, though, there really does seem to be something mystical about the way things turn out when Max has a hand in them.

Nortie showed a visible letdown when we split up, knowing he had to go back home to be with his mom and dad. I had a feeling he'd pay for being away. Lion came right out and offered to let Nortie live with him, but the vision of finishing out the year in a condemned apartment above a bar with a guy whose best and only housecleaning tool is a chisel steered Nortie back in the direction of home.

We knew we'd see each other plenty of times over the vacation, beginning with the Christmas dance that night at the Sheraton Ballroom, but we lingered a few minutes saying goodbye in the parking lot outside the Savage House, feeling the importance of this event.

I got home and called Devnee to be sure she knew what time I was picking her up and she sounded real excited and warm and I was glad I hadn't gone ahead and ended things. Besides, she makes me look like such a star, she's so pretty.

I was upstairs when Mom got home late in the afternoon from her bridge club, followed shortly by Dad from his Friday-afternoon poker game. They called me downstairs and asked if I'd had a good time at Stotan Week. I searched their faces and they looked to be sincere, and I decided not even to try. I said yes, I'd had a good time at Stotan Week. There was a time I tried to include my mom and dad in my life and got real frustrated because I didn't think they could understand what I was about. Now I know they can't understand what I'm about and I accept that and I don't get frustrated. They're more like sweet grandparents who are glad I don't get into a lot of trouble. I think as I get older I'm better able to respect where they've been, and their need to protect the comfort and calmness they have in their lives now. When I was a freshman on the Montana road trip, I got to bitching about them being old and uninvolved, and wondering out loud whether they ever touched each other or got "frisky," as they say on *Happy Days,* and Max said an interesting thing. He said part of the reason there's a "generation gap" is there's so much more information available to us than there was to our parents—and that will be true for our kids too. Max said he thinks we all do the best we can in our time with what we have, and that kids would be a lot more at peace with adults if they could understand that. When I look back at Mom and Dad through that light, it allows me to respect them more and need less. That's what killed Long John's relationship with them; Dad was a World War II bomber pilot and Long John was a Viet Nam War hippie-dippie glue-sniffing draft-evader, and there wasn't the chance of the lead lemming on a high cliff that either would ever see where the other was coming from. They solved it by simply dissolving the father-son relationship. Simple as that. I don't want that to happen with me. Besides, there are worse things than living with nice old people who let you do anything you want.

Mom and Dad offered me my choice of their cars for the dance to class up my act a little and I accepted Dad's RX-7, which allowed me to offer my car to Lion in case his date didn't have a mountain tent to keep her warm in his open-air Jeepster. Lion was indignant. "They take me for what I am," he said, assuming a Napoleonic pose and sucking in his cheeks.

"I guess that's better than taking you for what you've got," I said, and told him if he changed his mind, I'd leave it parked in the driveway with the keys in it.

The dance was great. I took Devnee to the roof of the Ridpath Hotel for dinner; it has a real nice view of the city and is formal and grownup and treats you like you are too. I don't know whether or not it's the best food in town, but that didn't matter because I'd been eating peanut-butter and scrambled-egg sandwiches all week and my taste buds were decimated.

Devnee looked *good*. She wore this kind of simple white short formal with a medium-low-cut V-neck that had me craning my neck every time she wasn't looking. Boy, I wish all a girl had to be was pretty, because I'd never consider anyone but her if that were true. We had a nice talk about nothing in particular and showed up at the dance early so we could watch everyone else come in.

Jeff and Colleen came about a half-hour later and that was a show-stopper. Something about being in real civilization down at Stanford hadn't hurt Colleen a bit. She just flat looked classy, and about ten years older than any of us except Jeff, who was decked out in his Marine Corps dress blues with the high collar and bright red stripe down the side of the pants. I was almost afraid to approach them; they looked like the King and Queen of Spokane.

And then Serbousek. You had to be somewhere near the door or outside to really appreciate Lion's entrance. And you'd also need to know a little more about his Jeepster. This thing was new back in the fifties and was kept in immaculate condition by his dad right up until he died. Lion still keeps it in great running condition, but he's altered its appearance considerably. Two years ago, in his World War II surrealistic period, Lion turned his Jeepster into a German WWI fighter plane. It's bright red with an Iron Cross on each door, and he has what appears to be a machine gun mounted on a tripod just behind the seat. There is also a winch on the front, should he nose-dive into any ditches. Anyway, when the Jeepster is in full dress, with the machine gun mounted and all, like on the night of the Christmas dance, Lion wears this hideous old floor-length fur coat and cloth WWI pilot's helmet, complete with goggles and a long scarf around his neck that whips along behind him in the wind.

He pulled up in front of the Sheraton, leaped over the door, danced around the Jeepster to take his date's hand— Marley Sharp is her name—and brought her to the ground as if he were helping her out of a stagecoach. He kissed the back of her hand lightly, then led her just inside the door, asked her to wait right there, my dear, and strode back to his craft. He waved to the crowd, flipped the scarf once around his neck and taxied down the runway toward the parking lot. In seconds he was back, minus the coat and helmet, looking spiffy as they come in a burgundy tux with a full-ruffled front and cuffs. As always, the crowd cheered.

Inside, Lion and Marley joined Jeff and Colleen and

Devnee and me at our table, at which time I subjected his outrageous formal wear to somewhat closer scrutiny.

"Lemme see your socks," I said.

Lion smiled. He pulled up his pant leg to reveal a near-perfect match to the dark burgundy pants.

"Couldn't get it exact, huh?" I said.

Marley looked confused. "Don't socks come with the tux, Lion?"

Come to light another of Lion's barbaric customs. Lion has been at war with society about socks since I can remember. He doesn't wear them; says his feet can't breathe. "Feet that smell like yours don't need to breathe," Jeff says, but Lion is unmovable on the subject of socks. Lion's socks at the Christmas dance were made by the same company from whom he buys the rest of his oil paints. As I would have expected, even though I didn't know her, Marley thought that was great. You don't go out with Lion unless you have at least a minimal taste for the outrageous.

The band was perfect. They played hard-core rock and roll and took short breaks, and we worked *out*. At the end of the second set I spotted Nortie over by the door, dressed in a sports coat and tie, with Milika holding his arm with both hands, anxiously looking around. I figured they must be looking for us, and I waved. He didn't see me at first, so I yelled. Milika moved toward us, sort of dragging Nortie a couple of steps behind. As they got closer, I could see that one side of Nortie's face was puffy and red and his eye was swollen almost shut. One hand absently held his ribs, but he seemed to be feeling no pain. In fact, he seemed gone. Devnee and I met them at our table; the others were circulating. They sat down and Nortie sort of smiled and nodded, the left side of his smile drooping beneath the weight of the damage. Milika's eyes were red and her face was streaked with tears.

"Your dad?" I said, and Nortie just looked at me.

"His dad found out about us," Milika said. "Marty O'Brian called and told him. Nortie called me from a telephone booth a few hours ago and asked me to come pick him up. I found him wandering around about a block from the booth. Something's wrong with him, Walker."

Nortie just looked over at Milika, then back at me. He smiled his creepy smile again and said, "Nothing's wrong," and sort of drifted away.

Lion and Jeff came back and sat down—in the first instant, real glad to see Nort, then shocked, and pissed. Nortie responded to them the same way he did to me. I thought maybe he had a concussion, but Lion took one look and said, "Nortie, what are you on?"

Nortie looked back and smiled. He shook his head slowly and laughed. "I'm not on anything," he said, and his words trailed off with his eyes.

Lion walked around the table and squatted in front of him, grabbing him by the shoulders. Nortie flinched a little, but smiled again and said, "You can go ahead and hit me. Nothing hurts."

Lion shook him. "Nortie, what are you on?"

Nortie shrugged again and said he didn't know.

Milika took his arm and turned his head toward her. "Come on, baby," she said. "Tell Lion what you took."

Nortie shook his head again. "I don't know," he said. "He didn't tell me."

I said, "Who didn't tell you?"

"Long John," he said. "Your brother, Walk. Isn't Long John your brother? He gave it to me. He said it would make me not hurt." He nodded his head and his eyes drooped. "He was right. He was right. I don't hurt."

I flipped Devnee my keys and said, "You guys get him up to Sacred Heart Emergency. We'll go find out what he took. If any of the chaperones give you trouble, tell them you think he hurt his head. *Don't* say anything about drugs."

We were halfway to the Rooster in Lion's Jeepster when I realized I'd forgotten my coat and would probably arrive there in need of medical treatment for hypothermia. Lion reached under his seat and handed me an old Army blanket, but I waved it off. Never mind what I thought may be living in there, I wanted to be cold and miserable and pissed when I saw my brother. I've always kept the seedier part of his life as far away from me as I could, and, to be honest, never really think about it, but if my brother's going to start peddling drugs to my friends, I'm going to kick his butt.

Jeff was in the back seat with the make-believe machine gun, and his was the voice of reason. "What are you figuring to do when we get there, Walk?"

"Find out what my brother gave Nortie, then rip his head off."

Jeff said, "Bad plan. The Rooster's a biker bar."

"I pull my brother out of there all the time," I said. "We'll be okay."

"You pull your brother out of there because they *let* you pull your brother out of there," he said. "If you want to help Nortie out, just find out what he took and we'll get out of there."

We pulled up in front of the Rooster and were out of the Jeepster almost before it stopped. There was a good-sized crowd and when we walked through the door in our fancy duds the whole place turned to look. For a split second I pictured leaving naked. Jeff was right, and I could see it, looking at their faces: these guys aren't to be messed with. All the karate moves in the world won't make up for how mean they can be. The bartender was a new guy and he came around the bar to meet us near the door. I caught a glimpse of Long John sitting in a booth over by the pool table with some guy who looked like he could eat a medium-sized shopping mall.

The bartender said, "I'll need to see some ID, guys," then looked us over. "Even if you have it, this might not be the place you're looking for."

"No ID," I said. "I'm John Dupree's brother. I need to talk to him for a minute. It's an emergency."

The bartender said he didn't know him, and I pointed him out. Long John hadn't seen us yet; he was lost in negotiations. "Could you just tell him I need to see him for a second?" I said. "We'll stay right here."

The two guys playing pool at the nearest table stopped and leaned on their cues, watching us. Lion and Jeff stood just behind me, trying not to give off anything that would heat the place up at all. With Lion decked out in his fur coat, they looked like a Marine and a bear. I wondered how bikers take to warriors and furry animals. Before the bartender could get Long John, one of the bikers nearest his booth elbowed him in the shoulder and pointed to us. Long John excused himself and came over. He moved through the crowd with that sort of laid-back saunter of his and that stupid grin he gets when he's high, and I wanted to break his neck.

"Nice threads," he said, and ran his fingers inside the lapel of my tux. "What're you doin' here? You guys didn't decide to have your prom at the old Rooster, did you?" He laughed at the idea, and a little spittle ran down his chin.

I said, "What did you give Nortie?"

"Your little swimmer friend?" he asked. "Jesus, his daddy's a mean one. You see that little bugger's face?"

"Yeah, I saw his face," I said. "What did you give him?"

"Can't remember for sure," Long John said. "Something for pain."

I started to grab him, but Jeff's hand came down on my arm. The guys at the pool table leaned their cues against the wall and moved over toward us. Jeff told Lion to go out and start the Jeepster. For the first time I realized how far in over our heads we really were and I calmed right down, but a little late. The pool-players and the guy in Long John's booth moved in, all three of them huge, with bushy beards, and chains hanging from their belts, and arms as big as my neck. The guy from Long John's booth had at least one tattoo for every day he'd been alive. Long John looked over at them; he seemed to sway a little. "It's all right, guys. This here's my brother. Been to the prom. He's my brother. It's all right." He looked at Jeff and me again. "Don't you guys have dates?"

I heard the Jeepster roar outside and knew Lion was ready for the getaway. I said, "Can you just give me a second with my brother? Just a second? It's important."

The guy who had been at Long John's booth grabbed my arm. "You got one minute," he said. "Talk to him and get out of here. You don't belong here. Any trouble and the lights go out." He backed off a little.

Long John said, "You shouldn't have come here, little brother. You should only come here when I call for you."

"I can see that," I said in a low voice. "Look, just tell me what you gave Nortie."

He said, "I don't know. I just saw him and he looked so *bad*. Made me feel bad, so I gave him something. I can't remember what. I was pretty messed up."

99

I nodded and got real close to him. "You aren't my brother. Next time you need to call someone to bail you out, you call somebody who gives a damn. You give that crap to my friends and you're not my brother. And there's no way back in. That's it. I don't even know you." I stepped back and smiled at the bikers, my heart pounding like a jackhammer, and motioned Jeff toward the door. He was more than ready to leave. I took a step back and fired a roundhouse at Long John with everything I had. It caught him flush on the side of the jaw, lifting him right off the ground. I didn't see him land; we were out the door and fishtailing down the block before those guys even moved.

"No luck," I said to Lion in the Jeepster. "Better go up to Sacred Heart."

Nortie looked a lot better when we got up there. They didn't think he had overdosed, but they pumped his stomach anyway, which is worse than getting beat up. I explained to the doctor why Nortie's face looked like someone had kicked their way out from inside his head; he said he was required to notify Child Protective Services, but when I told him Nortie is eighteen, he said Nortie would have to take legal action if he wanted the law involved. I know Nortie well enough to know that will never happen, so I decided Nortie didn't live with his mom and dad anymore and Jeff and Lion and I headed over to his place to get his stuff.

I was ready for anything when we got to the Wheelers' house—I've seen Mr. Wheeler at his worst—but Lion and Jeff were so hot the only thing we really had to worry about was whether or not one or both of them would go semiconscious and trash the place. It was nearly midnight, but the living-room light was on, and when we knocked, Mrs.

Wheeler answered in her bathrobe. Lion said, "We're here to get Nortie's things," and she moved aside and let us in. Nortie's dad met us in the doorway between the kitchen and living room and asked what the hell we thought we were doing. Lion said the same thing he'd said to Mrs. Wheeler and started to push past. I said before, Mr. Wheeler's not a big guy, and it's one thing for him to lose his temper and do Nortie or Mrs. Wheeler in, but quite another to take on someone with the size and temperament of Lion. And the real danger was with Jeff, who hadn't said a word yet.

When Mr. Wheeler went to the phone, Jeff did say a word. "Calling the cops?" he asked. "Emergency is 911. Tell them to get over here so we can talk about assault charges. If they want to pick up the evidence on the way, Nortie's up at Sacred Heart Emergency." He started into Nortie's room, then turned around in the doorway. "And tell them to hurry, because if you make the wrong move, there'll be more assault charges."

Nortie's dad stopped dialing and placed the receiver back in the cradle. We went on into Nortie's room to clean it out. Jeff dumped his clothes into two suitcases and a big box he found in the closet, while Lion started dismantling his stereo. I took his posters off the wall and picked up all the little knickknacks on the tops of the tables and dressers. When we had it all together and were ready to haul it out to the car, I looked up and there was good old Mr. Wheeler standing in the doorway with a pistol. Everything in me froze.

"You're in my home," he said. "You don't break into a man's home and start taking things." Advantage, Mr. Wheeler. That changed the tenor of things. Jeff slowly set the box he had down on Nortie's bed and showed his

---

palms. Lion did the same. All I remember thinking was: that's a gun. Guns put holes in things.

Mr. Wheeler kept it leveled. "You boys get out of here. Leave Nortie's things where they are and get the hell out of my house."

Mr. Wheeler turned to walk out of the room just as his wife came up behind him and saw the gun. She shrieked and went off into some other world. "No!" she screamed. "No! You're not shooting anyone! You can beat me and you can lock me in the basement and you can do anything you want, but you're not killing anyone! You'll have to kill me first! You're not shooting anyone! You're not shooting anyone. . . ."

At first Mr. Wheeler was taken aback, sort of stunned, but then he yelled at her to shut up. When she wouldn't, he reached out and backhanded her with the hand that held the gun. She dropped to the floor and lay still.

A wave of nausea swept through me and I thought I'd throw up right there on the floor. I hated Mr. Wheeler's guts and I wanted to kill him, but my fear of getting shot far outweighed my contempt for him, or my compassion for his wife, and I backed out. Lion and Jeff followed.

We got into the Jeepster shaking with fear and rage. Lion shoved it into gear and we roared down the block, took a hard right and headed up the arterial back to the hospital. About halfway there we started to pass a Union 76 station, and Lion swerved in. "Who's got a quarter?" he said, and I flipped him one. He stepped into the phone booth by the curb and dialed Wheeler's number. We crowded around him.

When Mr. Wheeler answered, Lion said, "Mr. Wheeler, this is Lion Serbousek. Don't hang up." Silence; but the line remained open. Lion said, "In thirty minutes we're going to drive by your house to pick up Nortie's stuff. If it's not out in front, we'll call the cops, and I swear to God we'll make enough noise that even if they don't arrest you, you'll be all over the front page of tomorrow's paper. They'll call you a wife-beater and a child-abuser and your stock in this town won't be worth dog crap." Still silence; still the line remained open.

Jeff took the phone from Lion and said, "Let me talk to Mrs. Wheeler." We were all relieved to hear her voice; I thought she was dead for sure.

Jeff said, "Mrs. Wheeler, we're coming by to get Nortie's stuff; your husband's going to put it outside for us. We're going to pick you up too."

She was crying, but said, "No, I'm okay. I'll be fine."

Jeff shook his head. "No. If you're not out front with Nortie's stuff, I'm calling the cops. The only way you can keep all this quiet is to be there. If you don't have a friend to stay with, we'll take you to the Battered Women's Shelter. My mom does volunteer work there; she can get you in."

She protested again, but Jeff cut her off. "You come with us, or we call the cops." He hung up.

Talk about up in the air. I had no idea whether Mr. Wheeler would comply or not, or if maybe he'd hole up in an upstairs room and pick us off as we came down the block. I knew for sure we could take Mrs. Wheeler anywhere we wanted and she'd be back home before we got three blocks away; but what the hell, sometimes even though you can't change things, you need to make a statement.

We drove around awhile, then, when the half-hour had passed, turned onto Wheeler's block. The dark silhouette of a pile of boxes shadowed the sidewalk, and Mrs. Wheeler sat on one of them, crying. The house was dark. We loaded everything and she gave us directions to a friend's house. I walked her to the door and waited for someone to answer. Mrs. Wheeler had called ahead; her friend put an arm around her and they disappeared inside.

So that was the first night after Stotan Week. Funny: you walk down the street or through a shopping mall or a grocery store and look at people's faces and wonder what their lives are like—at least, I *think* I'm not the only one who does that—and you can't imagine some of the horror that goes on; but they just go on looking like everything's okay. I mean, Nortie and his mom look like regular people most of the time. It must take a lot of courage to pull that off. It seems so *crazy,* yet it's happening to regular people. I mean, a reasonably intelligent woman goes back to a man who *beats her up two or three times a week*—and beats her up *bad.* And she doesn't go back just once; she goes back and goes back and goes back. And if someone told you a story about a kid who lost his brother to suicide just because the brother's life was so horrible there was no other way out and that kid has the exact same life, you'd think he was absolutely off his nut not to haul his butt out of there first chance he got. And if you heard that he not only stayed, but lied and told stories to explain away cuts and bruises and lumps to protect the guy who was giving them to him, you'd just call the men in the Funny Truck. But that's Nortie. And I know Nortie, and I know he's not crazy. But I also know there's something about human beings that I don't get, and sometimes I feel like it's the most important thing in the world to understand, and sometimes I wouldn't touch it with a ten-foot pole.

CHAPTER 9

Still January 2

So now Nortie lives with me. He's got Long John's old room and somehow that seems appropriate. I picked him up from the hospital the next morning and took him to my place, where my mom took one look at his face and said, "I always thought your father was a little rough." She nodded slowly. "You can stay here as long as you like." She better be careful; this is a pretty comfortable place. Nortie could be here till he's thirty-five.

A couple of nights after he moved in, I think it was Christmas Eve, Nortie came into my room with that somber look that tells you he's about to make things rough on himself again. He said, "You know, I broke the Athletic Code."

I said, "I know. Forget it."

"I don't know if I can," he said.

"I could beat it out of your head."

There's a clause in the Frost High School Athletic Code that says anyone using alcohol or non-prescriptive drugs when their sport is in season is automatically dropped from that sport for the remainder of the year.

"Extenuating circumstances," I said. "Forget it. Nobody needs to know. This is your captain speaking."

"What do you think Max would say to that?" he asked.

"Let's do Max a favor and not present him with that dilemma."

Nortie shook his head. "I don't know, Walk. Max is tough on me, but he's always been straight. I should be straight with him."

It's strange. As wild as we get sometimes, we've all tried hard not to break the Athletic Code. Sure, we have a few beers now and then, and I suppose a couple of us have tried grass, but never in season, and never to excess. If Max has taught us anything, he's taught us that our bodies have to carry us around a long time and we damn well better take care of them. Besides that, whether you agree philosophically with everything in the Code or not, you agree in writing if you want to play the sport. Big lesson in responsibility there: screw up and you're gone. Your choice. But here's Nortie, who's never had more than half a beer at one sitting and who trains like a man possessed, and I just don't think the Athletic Code was directed at what had happened to him over those past few days.

"I bought street drugs," he said, "and I took 'em. I at least need to tell Max."

"Nortie, why do you always have to make things worse than they already are?" I said. "Think of it as something that would be a pain in the butt for Max to know. He doesn't need to be bothered by something that isn't going to happen again in a million years. God, you're turning into an old lady."

"I'm blessing you with the ability to go back in time,"

Max said to Nortie two days later when he'd listened to Nortie's sordid story. We sat in the living room of Max's apartment drinking hot chocolate and eating Montana Christmas cookies. Max's mom still loves him. "You're going to travel back to the moment you got it in your pea brain to come tell me. And you're going to decide not to."

Nortie looked at him, then to me. I raised my eyebrows and shrugged as if to say, See, you little loon, what did I tell you?

Nortie looked back to Max, who is usually a stickler for rules and responsibility.

"Rules have a purpose," Max said. "That particular rule is to make athletes think twice before getting into habits that are going to put them in a bad way. The nature of what happened to you had nothing to do with that. It would be pointless to punish you." Max smiled. "And I don't want to have to explain that to my colleagues, so you didn't tell me. Drink your hot chocolate."

Nortie seemed pretty happy with Max's response—and surprised. The significant adults in Nortie's life so far hadn't exactly been understanding. In Nortie's world there were "No excuses, sir" right before he got cuffed alongside the head. But he wasn't really out to destroy his swimming career, and if Max said it was okay, it was okay.

We left Max's and went back to my place to change into our sweats and run an eight-miler. The temperature outside was in the teens, so we added extra layers of sweats and dug out some old stocking caps and mittens. Two or three inches of new snow covered the ground, and the going was easy—no slipping and sliding like in the past two days, when the cold had turned the streets to an icy glare and it was all we could do to stay vertical. We ran two or three miles along High Drive, overlooking the Pullman highway, then cut down through the neighborhoods bordering Manito Park. The light snow clung to the trees in the park like frosting, and ours were the first and only footprints along several of the back streets. Kids slid down the hills in the park on plastic garbage bags, squealing and yelling as the snow packed harder and harder and the rides got faster and faster. If you were going to make a postcard of Spokane to entice your relatives in Yuma, Arizona, to the great Northwest, you'd have taken the picture for it right there in the park.

When we turned the corner at the far north end of the park, ready to head back for the house, I spotted Marty O'Brian's pickup moving slowly along the edge of the street. At each house a rolled-up paper flew out the passenger's window onto the porch. I cut a wide circle onto one of the lawns and picked one of them up and, sure enough, it was the latest edition of the *Aryan Press*. We picked up the pace a little to catch him, and when we got close I could see through the back window that John Dolan, the team shortstop and relief pitcher, was throwing the papers out as O'Brian slowed for each house. I got even with John's window just as he fired a paper toward yet another lawn, caught it about a foot outside his window and winged it right back in, catching him hard on the side of the head. It took them both a second to realize what had happened, then O'Brian slammed on the brakes. The pickup slid several feet, almost out of control, before coming to a stop with the wheel against the curb. I put my elbows in through the window, resting my chin on my arms, with a big grin. "Marty!" I said. "What a surprise. I didn't know you had a paper route. Making some extra Christmas money? Christmas is over."

Marty flashed me the famous middle digit and Dolan threw the paper back at my head. I let it bounce off, and seriously considered reaching into the cab and feeding him the remaining papers. Dolan must have had an instinctive reaction to my hitting him with the paper. He wouldn't take me on. I said, "Dolan, you're not big or mean enough to have done that. I accept your apology." He didn't say anything.

O'Brian is another story. He and I have been on a collision course since Junior High. He said, "Get your elbows off my pickup, Dupree."

I ignored him. "This why you were so interested in Constitutional rights the day this garbage showed up at school?" I asked. "You're skating on pretty thin ice, O'Brain." It pisses him off when I call him O'Brain.

Marty started the pickup again and shoved it in gear. "Mind your own business, Dupree," he said, "and get off my pickup."

After the bikers in the Red Rooster and Nortie's armed father, O'Brian didn't seem scary. "Tell you what, Marty. I don't know why you're delivering these—I find it difficult to believe that even you are dumb enough to believe what's in them—but if I see one more of them fly out the window of this here pickup, I'm going to break out all your windows."

O'Brian sneered. "You think you're pretty hot stuff with all that karate crap, don't you, Dupree? Well, you don't scare me, man. One of these days you and me are going to see what's what."

"We'll see right now if you throw out one more of those papers," I said.

"Yeah, well, we're done delivering for today anyway, but one of these days . . ."

I said, "It probably won't be the biggest mistake of your life, O'Brain, but it'll be your biggest one this year."

He laughed. "You talk good," he said, then leaned forward and looked past me to Nortie, who was standing on the sidewalk. "Hey, Wheeler. Nice shiner you got there. Somebody finally tell your daddy you been sweet on a little jungle bunny?"

I shot over Dolan to grab him, but couldn't quite reach him, and he hit the gas, laughing and slapping me away. Even *I'm* smart enough not to get caught half in and half out of a moving vehicle, so I pushed myself back and slid to the ground; but I was plenty pissed. I swore I'd get even with O'Brian in a big way, but he just laughed more and fishtailed away. I made a quick snowball and fired at his rear window, but the snow was too cold and light, and it disintegrated in thin air.

"How'd he know you'd get your butt kicked if he told your old man about Milika?" I asked.

"Remember the day those papers showed up at school?"

I said I remembered.

"Well, the reason I didn't come out and raise hell with you guys is because I see them all the time. My dad gets them. I think he pays dues to those people. I didn't come out because I was embarrassed. Anyway, if O'Brian's delivering them, my dad probably knows him."

We turned onto the arterial that runs back up to High Drive. "Well," I said, "Max is probably right. If we raise a stink, it only makes them look like they have a point. When I finally get a chance to beat what few brains O'Brian has to putty, I should think of a different reason."

We ran up the arterial in silence, really putting on the pressure through the incline, subscribing to the age-old coaching adage that if it hurts, it must be good for you.

When we reached the top of the arterial and leveled off back onto High Drive, Nortie took a deep breath and blew out hard. "Could I ask you a question?" he gasped.

"Shoot."

"You sleep with Devnee?"

"You can ask," I said. "I won't promise an answer."

"Bad question?"

"It's a great question," I said. "It's just none of your business. Why do you want to know?"

"Milika wants to sleep with me," he said.

I started to laugh, which is not a good thing when you're out of breath. "All right!" I said. "I bet you won't get much sleep, though."

"I don't get any sleep just thinking about it," he said. "Promise you won't tell if I tell you something?"

"Sure."

"I'm scared to do it." He shook his head. "I keep thinking up excuses not to, but I'm running out."

I said, "Well, I don't have any ready-made excuses for not sleeping with your girlfriend, but I'll tell you something that might help."

"Tell it."

"It's a secret about males in the human race under the age of eighteen," I said.

"What?"

"We all say we're doing it, and almost nobody is. The plain, simple, ugly truth is we're most of us whacking away alone at home."

"You think so?" he said. He sounded hopeful.

"Check the math. If all the guys who say they're getting laid are really getting laid, and all the girls who say they aren't aren't, then there are three or four hundred guys making it with about six girls. Relax, we're all virgins."

"You're not sleeping with Devnee, are you?"

"I'm not sleeping with Devnee," I said. "And if I ever do, I'm not gonna sleep much either."

Nortie laughed, then thought a minute. "I don't like it

when guys talk about making it with someone—whether they are or not. Especially when they aren't. I mean, most of the time the girl never even has a chance to deny it, because she doesn't know it's being said."

"I guess Elaine has a cure for that," I said, and Nortie just nodded in agreement. That's an understatement, and Nortie knew exactly what I was talking about.

I was walking down the hall one morning between second and third periods when a voice behind me said, "Boy, I'd like to get a piece of that." I looked up to see Elaine walking down the hall the other way, and when I turned around I saw the voice came from none other than Fartin' Martin O'Brian. The guy with him—the same guy who was delivering papers with him that day, John Dolan—said, "I already did, man."

O'Brian punched him in the shoulder. "Right. I'll bet. You couldn't get a piece of a hollow log."

"No, really," Dolan said. "She acts cool, but she's as hot for it as any other chick. I didn't even have to do anything. She was all over me."

There was a pause. "You kidding me?" O'Brian said finally. It's amazing how easy it is to believe something we want to believe.

Dolan raised his right hand. "Last year. It's the gospel," he said. "Take her out. See for yourself."

I wanted to turn around and tell them both that if either one of them tried to take Elaine out, she'd tear them a new anal orifice, but I let it pass. O'Brian said he might just do that and I walked away from their stupid conversation. That was the first time I had any idea how degrading it is for guys to make up stories about who they've been in the sack with. It's a lot clearer when it's someone you know.

Anyway, the next day we were all in Dolly's after school. It was springtime; swimming season was over and we were on the prowl. Dolan walked in and sat down at a booth with O'Brian and a bunch of the other baseball players; they had just finished practice, I think. I kicked Elaine under the table and said, "Hey there, hot stuff. I hear you're pretty good in the sack."

A quick confused look passed over her face, like she couldn't believe I'd said that, followed by another look that said: How would you like to have to go through your stools to count your teeth?

I put my hands in the air and said, "Just repeating what I heard." I repeated Dolan and O'Brian's conversation for her.

Elaine pursed her lips and her eyes narrowed. "I did go out with him," she said, "for the same reason I give quarters to bums on the street. The jerk took me to Five-Mile and gave me the old 'put out or get out' routine." She laughed. "I punched him in the chest as hard as I could and got out. He followed me all the way back to the city apologizing and begging me to get back in. Took me almost two hours to walk home."

For a few minutes Elaine watched Dolan yucking it up and being cool with his buddies, then she said, "Excuse me a minute."

She walked over to their booth and pulled up a chair. Dolan was resting his arm on the table and she elbowed it off. "John, you big stud," she said. "How you doin'?"

Dolan just looked at her funny.

"Heard you think I'm pretty good in the sack," Elaine said. "Couldn't get me off you, huh?"

Dolan looked at her, then back to his buddies, finding himself desperately short on conversational skills. I can't believe it, but I started to feel sorry for him.

Elaine said, "You know, it's funny, John, but I can't remember. Hard to believe I'd forget something that electrifying. You wouldn't happen to have a teensy-weensy little thing, would you? I can see how I'd forget that. Or maybe you were a little quick on the trigger. I *know* I'd forget that."

At this point Dolan knew the only way out was straight up, and his cronies were starting to snicker and turn away.

Then Elaine stuck her index finger right in the middle of his chest. Hard. She said, "John Dolan, you know as well as I do I wouldn't have sex with you if you were the nearest thing to a human being left on this earth. You should be really careful what you say, because you can end up looking like a fool." Then she looked over to O'Brian and said, "Not in my worst nightmare, Marty. Not in my worst nightmare." She scooted her chair back and came back over to our booth.

Lion stood up and clapped. A couple of the baseball players did the same and there was plenty of hooting. Dolan stayed a few minutes to see if there was any way to save face, found none, and split. When he got up to leave, O'Brian said in a voice that could be heard all over the restaurant, "See you later, you big stud, you," and laughed like a hyena.

I didn't have as much contempt built up for Marty then as I do now, but I remember thinking I wouldn't like very much to have him as my friend in a pinch.

Nortie and I took off our running shoes and sweatsocks in the mudroom just off the kitchen and hustled through the house upstairs to the shower. The bottoms of our sweatpants were hard as rocks and Nortie was teasing about having to break his off. My folks were gone wherever it is they go in the afternoons, so I cranked up the Kingston Trio till we could hear it in the bathroom. Just because I'd written Long John off didn't mean I had to write off the Kingstons. Nortie took the first shower and I sat on the toilet with the lid down, reading the paper and enjoying the warm steam.

"You think Jeff and Colleen sleep together?" he asked.

The headline on the front page was about some guys linked to the Aryan Nations who were running around the country knocking over banks and Brinks trucks to get money to gather weapons. They sounded like a bunch of loons, even though the quotes indicated they took themselves pretty seriously. I wondered if O'Brian knew what a jerk he looked like, being a delivery boy for them.

"I don't have a count on who's sleeping with who," I said, popping to.

Nortie said, "I know, but just tell me about Jeff and Colleen."

"Jeff *better* be sleeping with her," I said. "I ran with him yesterday and he almost didn't make the full eight miles. He *really* slowed down after five. He's getting worn down *somewhere.*"

I was reminded that I'd actually been a little worried about Jeff at the end of our run. He's in great shape; eight miles is nothing. But he really was sucking at the end. Not out of breath, just tired. Anyway, I ran with him again three or four days later and he seemed just fine.

So we're back in school and ready to start the season in earnest. We'll travel at least three weekends out of four until early March, which is when the State meet is held in Seattle. I'm going to try to let *nothing* interrupt my concentration on swimming between now and then. That is, I *was* going to try. Today in English class I heard that Elaine went to the Christmas dance with a guy named Peter Wilson, who's the student teacher in my Government class. They must have shown up after we left. I wonder why she didn't mention it. I sure didn't need to know it.

CHAPTER 10

January 21

We got back into workouts, and back into school, no sweat. It's funny, we get our best grades in-season. I think that's because we know we don't have any time to screw around. We're working out four to five hours a day, and it takes another hour and a half to get the sting of the chlorine out of our eyes; we're all throwbacks—none of us uses goggles. Add to that the amount of sleep we need to operate at this pace and about all that's left is time for epic meals and schoolwork. Procrastinate on an assignment and you're lost. But when you get in this good a shape, I believe you think better. Your blood, stoked with oxygen and nutrients and brain food, shoots through your head like a river and you get twice the work done in half the time.

We're way ahead of schedule in our workouts. Except for Jeff, everyone's times have been dropping like a rock, and it's looking like we may qualify our 400 free relay for State.

Even though we're strong in different events, we're all strong 100 freestylers. What a coup that would be, to end the year winning something together. Of course, that depends on Jeff getting off his plateau. I'm sure he will; everyone hits one sometime—it's a curse of the sport—and Jeff's been a swimmer longer than any of us, actually, so he knows he can swim through it if he works his butt off and doesn't get down. He's as patient as they come. It's early in the season; the best time for it to happen if it has to happen at all.

Nortie's getting pretty used to living at our place. He had a hard time with it at first—always wanted to drive by his house to see if everything was all right. After a few midnight passes he finally figured out there's no way he can tell if everything's all right by just driving by, and no way he can make things all right under any circumstances. He meets with his mom downtown once a week for lunch and that helps some, though he says he'd like to contact his dad too. Mr. Wheeler's too pissed at him to make that possible; in fact, if he knew Mrs. Wheeler was seeing Nortie, he'd probably kick her butt. So, slowly but surely, he's getting used to the fact that nothing is going to change at his house and the best thing he can ever do is stay away and not fan the flames.

Nortie has also decided on a new and different life's work, now that he's convinced he's too dangerous a dude for the teaching profession. Nortie's now going to be a psychologist; and from what I've seen so far, someone should warn serious members of that profession that he's coming.

He caught me after we finished our homework last Tuesday night and wanted me to go over to school with him.

"What for?" I asked.

"Gotta go make Richard Nixon smarter," he said.

I said, "Better men have tried. What are you talking about?"

"Take me and I'll show you."

I got up. I'd finished a report for Government class on the Watergate affair and, clearly, any attempts to make Richard Nixon smarter couldn't hurt. I busted my butt to make the paper a good one to impress Mr. Wilson, the student teacher who took Elaine to the Christmas dance. Actually, "impress" might be the wrong word. I wanted him thinking I'm as smart as I am big and mean and good-looking, so if he ever has reason to mess with me, he won't. That's the grownup way to handle romantic wars.

"This better be good," I said, putting on my coat.

"It's good," Nortie said.

Nortie had talked Mr. Redden, the Psych teacher, out of a key to the school so he could get in at night to do lab work. Since we spend so much time out of school during swimming season, Nortie thought it would be a good idea to work after hours and stay caught up. Getting the key took an act of the School Board; there probably aren't three other kids in school who could have gotten it, but Nortie's one of those people everyone takes care of, and somehow Mr. Redden or Mrs. Stevens, the vice-principal, presented it right.

"We talking about Richard Nixon the fallen president?" I asked as we got out of the car and started down the hill toward the front entrance.

"Richard Nixon the rat," he said. "Jeff says they're one and the same. I'm missing two lab periods for the Montana road trip, so I need to get ahead. Come watch, it's kinda neat."

I said, "Hell, yes, I'll come watch. I didn't drive you all the way over here to wait out in the cold. Besides, not many people get the chance to educate a former President, though it might have done more good back in 1968."

Our feet crunched over the frozen snow covering glare ice. Nortie wore slick loafers and he handed me his notebook and took off running and skating to the bottom of the hill, screaming, "Henny Youngman!" as he tried a little pirouette. He landed on his butt.

"That's Sonja Henie," I yelled, "and she's a girl."

"Really?" he yelled back. "Dick Button, then."

In the Psych lab it smelled like maybe Richard Nixon and his cabinet had staged a poop-in. Nortie flipped on the light, went over to a stack of cages by the far wall, reached inside the one marked RICHARD NIXON—¾ and pulled out a little white rat. He petted Mr. Nixon a minute and talked politics, then placed him in a glass cage with several switches on the outside, a steel-gridded floor, a lever and a small receptacle inside at one end, with a closed container for pellets feeding into the receptacle.

"Your basic Skinner Box," Nortie said, peering through the glass at his rat, which impatiently pressed the lever and checked the tray. "He should have been a smarter president," Nortie said. "He remembers everything I taught him yesterday."

Richard Nixon pawed the lever a few more times, without result because Nortie wasn't ready yet, and sniffed around the Skinner Box. I looked around the lab at the other cages. Each rat's name was taped to the outside of its cage. There was Billy Sol Estes, Adolf Hitler, Macbeth and several other well-known scoundrels from the worlds of history and literature. "Named after other famous rats," Nortie said. "Mr. Redden's a funny guy."

"How come he doesn't have Percy Cerruti?" I asked.

Nortie's eyes brightened and he laughed out loud. He

walked over to Richard Nixon's cage and tore the taped name tag away, brought another tag out of Mr. Redden's desk and wrote Cerruti's name on it with a felt-tipped pen. "I'll make it legal in class tomorrow," he said.

He went back to his rat, which was sniffing aimlessly around the box, stopping to push the lever every so often without result.

"You taught him to hit the lever for food?" I asked.

"Yup. But I can teach him a lot more than that. Just watch. Spring term last year, Mr. Redden taught Benito Mussolini to press the bar, turn three full circles to the right, two full circles to the left, then hit the bar twice. He'd do that up to six times for one pellet. Mr. Redden said he could have made him do it a hundred times, but it was boring him to death. Benito willed his brains to science." Nortie activated his hand-held switch. "Watch, I'll show you how this works." Percy Cerruti had moved over to the other side of the box and Nortie waited for him to approach the receptacle. When he did, Nortie pressed the button and a pellet appeared. Percy recognized the click and was on the pellet like stink on poop, then immediately hit the lever. Another pellet. "I can make him hit it any number of times I want, just to get one pellet," he said. "I just gradually work up the number of times it takes to get one. If I put him on a Variable Interval Reinforcement Schedule—not let him know how many times he has to hit it—I can make him bang on that thing till his paw falls off."

"Maybe you should change his name back to Richard Nixon," I said. "Sounds like presidential material to me." I watched him for a couple of seconds, totally engrossed in what he was doing. "Nortie, you sure you want to do this for a living instead of teach? I mean, who you gonna work for, Barnum and Bailey?"

"I'd teach if I could," he said, "but this isn't so bad. I mean, a psychologist doesn't spend all his time training rats. This is how people learn too, you know."

"Really? Funny, I can't remember my time in a Skinner Box."

Nortie laughed. "Pretty cute. But really, Walk, the pellet is just reinforcement. It's something the rat really wants. You keep him hungry all the time so you know that. That's what the ¾ on the cage means; he's at three-fourths his natural weight. When you get him in the box, if you're patient, you can teach him anything just by knowing what he wants. If you can figure out what reinforces somebody, you can know a lot about them. Mr. Redden says we're just sophisticated rats."

I watched Cerruti jump through his hoops while Nortie recorded it all in his lab book and I couldn't help but wonder at the nature of the reinforcement that keeps Nortie wanting beyond anything to please a dad who beats him up and a mother who never protected him. I didn't ask.

"Mr. Cerruti's got you going pretty good too," I said after a while. "Look at you, stuck here at nine o'clock at night, pushing that button every time he hits the lever."

Nortie didn't even look up. "Yup," he said. "We both have to do it right if it's going to work. This here operant conditioning is mutual."

So Nortie has discovered the meaning of life and that's given him new focus. Sometimes I think any focus would do—that he just needs something to believe in and hungry white rats are as good as anything. Anyway, he's attached to his new life's work; and it sure isn't hurting his swimming any. He's been absolutely unbeatable the first two weeks of the season. So far he's swum different events in each meet—we've had three to date: one the first weekend and two the second—and in anything farther than 100 yards he's out of the water and half dry before the number-two man finishes. Lion's been amazing too. He's far ahead of his old times, particularly in the 'fly, and far ahead of where anyone would have predicted. Lion seemed to add all kinds of new fuel to his tanks the first day back to school when he walked up to Marty O'Brian and told him he couldn't care less what his political or religious beliefs were, but that if one more of those stupid Aryan papers showed up on our campus he would hold O'Brian personally responsible and would hurt him in ways O'Brian didn't know existed and after that would hand-deliver him to the Conners brothers, a couple of black linebackers on the football team, who would more likely than not spread his body parts evenly over the vast Inland Empire. O'Brian gave him some lip, but it was weak. My guess is that he'll cool it.

It's interesting: O'Brian uses his affiliation with those guys to express his distaste for blacks, but the Aryans spend most of their time on Jews and I don't think O'Brian knows enough about Jews to know what he's supposed to not like. I wonder how many people who hang out with them are just unconscious peckerheads who need someone to hate.

Anyway, the point was that Lion is getting *fast* and will probably qualify for State in the 100 'fly. Everything in Stotan land is perfect except for the fact that Jeff is stuck. He actually slowed a couple tenths of a second in the last meet down in Pullman, but I think that was due to a bad start and one mediocre turn.

This next weekend is Montana, and even though it's a driving marathon—we go to Billings, clear across on the eastern side of the state, and then up to Havre, close to the Canadian border—Lion and I are both going to try to qualify for State there. Because the high schools and colleges share the pool in both towns, we swim at Eastern Montana State's pool in Billings and Northern Montana's pool in Havre: both fast pools—particularly Northern's.

I think the Montana road trip, more than any other, makes us family. We're together from mid-afternoon on Thursday until way late Sunday night non-stop. That's like being in a sensory-deprivation tank with friends of Jabba the Hutt for three days. Swimming just wouldn't be the same without the Montana road trip.

CHAPTER 11

February 2

I qualified for State out of state—in Havre, Montana. Fourth meet of the year and I'm in—at least in the 500. I've never been this strong or in this good a shape. I just keep getting faster and there's no limit. I'm not lifting weights now, or doing any workouts other than in the water, and I've increased my daily mileage by about half. At the beginning of the year all I wanted to do was qualify again, or maybe dare to hope to make it to the consolation finals, but now I don't know; anything could happen.

Before my race in Havre, Max told me that after ten laps I should shoot for the level of fatigue I reached during the worst parts of Stotan Week. I didn't even get close—the race isn't long enough—but my time was more than three seconds below State qualifying time.

And it may not even matter.

This weekend I got a good look at a rough side of being a

human being on this planet, and things may never be the same again.

I said the Montana road trip is a bear, but we love it. Last year, even though he was out of school and not swimming, Jeff worked a way to get emergency weekend leave from his Reserve training to go along because it's such a good trip. It's the longest of the season, an infinity of driving and swimming and putting up with each other. Thursday afternoon we begin the 500-mile drive east to swim against the two high schools in Billings on Friday, then shoot another 400 miles north to take on the high school in Havre on Saturday. Sunday it's a straight shot back to Spokane. Most of the traffic we see is snowplows and sanding trucks; we could make the trip faster on a five-passenger dogsled, but the school doesn't have a dogsled, so we fill up the back of the van with oranges and candy bars and head for cowboy country.

Thursday we left an hour later than planned—Cerruti the rat got an extra hour of The Game of Life, which is what Nortie now calls the Skinner Box—in cold, clear, sunny weather amid high hopes of winning lots of races and losing two meets. Lion had T-shirts made up that said:

FROST
SWIMMING
We're Number Three

because there are usually two other teams at each meet.

We barely cross the border into the Idaho panhandle, headed up into the Rockies, before Jeff moves to the portable seat across from Nortie in the back of the van, takes Nortie's book out of his hand, closes it and starts to deal.

Nortie utters a weak "Help, help, save me," but three years of road-trip tradition will not be denied. There is no escape. Jeff has already informed Nortie they will be attending the same college so Jeff can work his way through playing Gin Rummy with him. It's doubly hard on Nortie because, besides losing nearly every hand, he has to suffer Jeff's derision every time he lays down a card that he'd have known better than to play had he been paying attention. Nortie never pays attention. "Were you gone to the bathroom when I played that?" Jeff says, or "Good to see you're saving threes. There's two more of them in the discard pile." Then when Jeff slaps his hand down on the seat, yelling, "Gin!" he sucks his tooth. Nortie dives for his coat, but if he makes it, Jeff blows the ill wind down the sleeve.

Lion's been quiet on this trip. He sketches most of the time we ride and comes to only when we stop to eat, though sometimes you can get him started on a monologue as he draws. Tonight he's not talking much. One of the Billings swimmers is a top-notch butterflyer and Lion is going to have to haul it out to beat him. His silence is a psych-up, though he'll get plenty verbal just before the race. We know he's feeling okay because he packs away everyone's extra fries and pickles and any other tidbit left unattended. He's also stocked the jukebox—a vintage Rock-Ola—with quarters and punched up every rock song in sight, some of them twice, in an effort to block out the other customers' selections, which seem to lean heavily to Tammy Wynette, George Jones and even Gene Autry. Some of the records were in there when this machine was made.

In an hour we're back in the parking lot, ready to forge on. Snow falls in tiny, feathery flakes and light wind sways the tall lodgepoles back and forth just at the edge of our vision behind the parking-lot spotlights. Off behind the restaurant somewhere a stream, surely outlined in icy white, tumbles over frozen rocks. Max stands beside the van, head cocked, listening and watching; this is home for him. He looks like he'd just as soon head into the little bar, order up a pitcher of beer and sit the rest of the night in front of the big stone fireplace that takes up most of one wall. But he makes a quick phone call on the pay phone just inside the door and we're off. We got places to go, butts to kick.

A half-hour back on the road, I offer Max a breather at the wheel so he can catch a little shut-eye and drive late. He decides it's a good idea and pulls over so we can switch. The snow isn't real bad, but it slows us some because I don't know the road as well as Max and I don't want to be the reason the Frost swimming team disappears from the face of the earth before achieving its appointed destiny.

The light in the back of the van is on and Lion still sketches, calling up to me to change the radio station once in a while and occasionally setting his work aside to stare out the back window into the snowy darkness. Nortie owes his net worth plus in gambling debts to Jeff, so they've shut down the game for the night. Max is supposed to be sleeping, but I see his reflection in the windshield, and he's awake, staring silently into the snow flying into our headlights, almost hypnotized. Who knows what he's thinking?

About three quarters down the east side of the mountains Max takes over again. I'm pretty sure he hasn't slept, but he says he's rested and wants me to get some sleep for the meet tomorrow. I settle in comfortably, back against the door, feet on the engine cover, and close my eyes. But it just ain't time for the kid to nod off. Watching Max's reflection in the windshield off the greenish glow of the panel lights, I notice what a handsome man he is. He's not classic, certainly not in our culture, but his look is strong—easily powerful. It's the handsomeness of wisdom and self-assurance. I find myself wishing I knew him better.

My wish is granted in a way I would never have expected. Somewhere in the eastern foothills, just before spilling out onto the Great Plains to begin the longest, flattest, most boring ride known to Western man, Max takes a sudden left onto a side road and drives about three miles till we come in sight of a small farmhouse. He turns again into the long driveway and pulls up next to the snowy front yard. Lion has long since hung up his sketching and sacked out. He sits up and looks around, then drops like a rock without even asking.

The living-room curtains part and a woman's face appears in the window; then below her, in the same window, a child peers out through cupped hands. Max reaches into the glove compartment, removes a pair of mittens and says, "Hang tough, I'll be back in a few minutes." It doesn't even occur to me to ask what we're doing here. Nortie wakes up and asks where we are and I tell him to go back to sleep. Jeff doesn't stir.

As Max approaches the house, the woman, dressed in a blue velour robe and sheepskin slippers, opens the front door and the little girl shoots past her and down the sidewalk in her snowsuit, arms wide open, takes a flying leap and engulfs Max. The woman disappears back inside, and for the next fifteen or twenty minutes I watch a different Max than I've ever seen. They romp in the snow, throw snowballs—only hers connect—make snow angels. Max carries her around the yard on his back, throws her into the snowbank and tickles her, all to the tune of her delighted squeals. Then they roll up three gigantic snowballs for a snowman, and when it's together, with two really stupid rocks for eyes and sticks for arms, Max lifts her up to put his hat on the snowman's head.

I'm completely struck that I'm watching Max Il Song romping and playing in the snow with a six-year-old girl in the wee hours of the morning in the middle of nowhere; and somehow I know it's important.

The door to the house opens and the woman stands in the doorway, arms folded, looking patient. Max and the little girl hug and he walks her back to the porch, exchanges a few words with the woman and turns to come back down the sidewalk as the two disappear. The little girl appears in the front window again and waves; Max waves back from the door of the van.

"Thanks for waiting," he says, sliding back into the driver's seat, like maybe I had a choice; like maybe I was going to drive off and leave him out there in the dead of night at the foot of the Rocky Mountains.

We drive in silence for the next half-hour or so. I wish I knew what I just saw, wish I could find a way to talk to him; but if he wanted to talk, he would. He just watches the snow-covered road and pushes on. He looks sad.

"That's what I like about athletics," Max said after a while, as if continuing a conversation we'd been having all along. "The rules are so clear. You know the consequences of every act: exactly how many fouls you get; what makes you a player and what takes you out of the game."

I didn't know what to say, so I nodded.

"That was my daughter," he went on, and I said, "Oh."

He was quiet a second, then he gave me a glimpse of what I might be in for if I want to grow up with anything that resembles grace. He said, "You know, Walker, I've worked real hard in my life to make sense of things. I studied Tai Kwan Do for years and years to teach myself discipline; spent a lot of time in the Orient trying to get some different perspectives—my ancestors' perspectives—and I think I've done a pretty good job of becoming conscious." He was quiet again and I thought I saw a tear in his eye. "I love Allysia like fury," he said; then with a half-smile. "Even more than her mother hates me. And it kills me that I can't be there for her during this time in her life, while she's growing up and changing every day and trying to make sense of things for herself."

I said, "I guess you don't get to see her very much."

"I see her when her mother says I can see her," he said, and obviously wasn't going into it further.

Max was quiet another mile or two, tapping his fingers against the wheel with a clicking sound I recognized—it was the first time I noticed he had bought himself a Stotan ring too—then he said, "You know, Walker, I'm not a bad man. I try to be straight and I think I'm pretty decent. But no matter how decent you are, no matter how intensely you work toward the light, nothing changes the past. This is a world where you pay for everything you do. Remember that. Life doesn't forgive you because you're young and ignorant. Life only has to be true to itself."

He looked over at me and smiled. "That doesn't mean you're supposed to live in fear. Just be sure to consider what you do."

"We're going to mix it up in Billings," Max announces about 10:30 Friday morning as we shoot east across the plains, having spent maybe three and a half hours in the Butte TraveLodge before getting up at 7:00 to push on. We're down out of the Rockies, we've had a good breakfast and we're making good time, with the sky only spitting and the loose snow swirling behind the van as we zero in on Billings. "Walker, you'll do the sprints."

I cheer. Trading the 50 and the 100 for the 200 and the 500 gives me a net gain of 550 yards.

"We swim at the college in Havre, and they've got the faster pool," Max goes on. "I want to rest you a little to hit the qualifying time there. Lion, you'll stay with the 'fly in Billings. Collins will push you good there." He smiles. "Now we need a volunteer for the distances."

"Jeff will do them," Nortie says.

Jeff looks asleep, but he squints one eye open and shakes his head slowly.

I say to Nortie, "If you want me to qualify on Saturday, you got to make sacrifices."

"You're right," Nortie says. "I'll sacrifice Jeff."

Jeff sucks his tooth. Nortie will swim the distances.

We talk strategy for a few miles. We'll swim the freestyle relay, forfeit the medley. Once again we'll lose the meet on second and third places, but we'll show well in our events.

We go back to what we were doing, the interior of the van bright from the reflection of the snow outside. Though the sky is still gray, you almost need sunglasses to watch the road or read.

Nortie explains to Jeff that if he could figure out what reinforces Jeff, he could train him to do anything Nortie wants. "You'd be my slave," he says. "No more of this big-red-bully stuff, no more Gin Rummy. You'd be licking my boots." Jeff sucks his tooth again and blows Nortie over. Lion draws a quick sketch of that, only in the picture Jeff's breath is a surly dragon, and Nortie applauds.

We drop the meet to both high schools in Billings, as expected, and blow them away doing it. Lion wins the 100

131

'fly and is within eight tenths of a second of qualifying time. We're in Billings long enough to swim, shower and get back on the road north to Havre. Jeff is down because his times were slower than last week, so there's no Rummy game. Darkness has already closed in as we pass the city limits and we figure we need to make it at least halfway before stopping. It's more two-lane highway a good deal of the way, but it's mostly flat and straight, so we make reasonable time. Max wants to give us a couple hours to stretch and warm up in Havre tomorrow, so we'll have another quick stay in some cowboy motel along the way and head out early.

I'm up front again with Max, and as we work our way north through the snowy night, I can't help wishing we could get back to that level of intimacy I felt with him last night. But that's over. There's no denial; Max isn't embarrassed or anything, just back to dealing with what's immediate. I can't help feeling privileged to have been given that glimpse through the window of his life.

After a short night in a one-horse motel in a one-horse town I never got the name of, we hit the road early and roll into Havre about 1:30 in the afternoon. That gives us two and a half hours before the meet, so we wander around town awhile, wondering if this is really the Yukon. We check into the Roundup, stretch out on the beds for fifteen or twenty minutes, then head over to the pool. We find we're going to be swimming against the college swim team too and they have two guys trying to qualify for small-college Nationals. That gives us something more to shoot for. You couldn't mix college and high-school athletes in most sports, but some of the fastest swimmers in the world have yet to see their first shaving razor, and even though we weren't notified ahead of time, Max thinks it's a great idea.

Since neither the high-school nor the college team has a real good middle-distance man, I'll have to do it on my own, but I swim well against the clock anyway. Max enters me in the 1,000—strictly a college distance—to get a good long warmup, and says to swim it about three-quarters speed. My 500 split in that is within four seconds of State qualifying time, so I know I'm hot. I feel strong as a bull. My 500 time is three seconds under what I need and Nortie jumps into the water, hugging me and splashing water on my face and yelling "Awright!" almost before I touch, and when I catch my breath I have to hold him underwater to calm him down. Max is right there with his stopwatch and a handshake.

Lion is two tenths closer in the 100 'fly and we figure he's got it made by next week, but the thing that makes it all academic is that Jeff collapses on the last lap of the 100 backstroke.

He goes out ahead for the first fifty yards, ready to blow it open after the second turn, then just runs out of gas. Near the end of the third lap everyone has passed him, and shortly after the turn into the fourth he gets caught up in the rope and can't get out. We watch in disbelief for a split second before Lion dives in and hauls him out. Jeff can't get it back; he's breathing short and looks pale and *real* disoriented. He lies on the deck awhile and we dry him off. Nortie's panicked, running around, trying to cover him with towels. Even the college trainer takes a look at him. Finally, to be safe, they call a local ambulance.

Boy, now that was scary. Jeff is the toughest guy I know, and watching him lying there on the deck with no control over anything wasn't my idea of a good time. We stuffed our clothes in our swimming bags and wore our warmups out of there. There was only the medley relay left, which we weren't swimming, and I don't think any of us could have swum anymore anyway, though I don't think anyone believed anything was seriously wrong. Max gave me the keys to the van and told me to go back to the Roundup; that he'd go with the ambulance and call us in my room as soon as he knew anything. By then Jeff had come to, though he looked real tired, and he said he was fine; he wanted to go back to the motel with us. Max said no deal and we split.

Back at the Roundup, we holed up in Nortie's and my room, eating chips and dip we got from the store across the street, watching the CBS Evening News on TV and waiting for Max to call. One of the lead stories was about more of those so-called neo-Nazis being arrested and connected to previously unsolved felonies all over the country, like bank robberies and armored-car holdups. It's kind of strange to see these guys on TV getting all this coverage. Even before the Aryan papers showed up at school—in fact, years before—we knew they were over at Falls Lake, but everyone I knew just thought they were a bunch of bozos whose IQs matched the number of letters in their middle initial, and who had nothing better to do than to sit over there figuring out who they hate. Now they're on national television and look legitimate. This world is not without its strangeness.

Nortie wondered out loud if his dad had ever knocked over a bank or a Brinks truck. "Shoot," he said, "when he was driving truck, he was gone all the time. Who knows what he was up to?" Nortie's getting a *little* bit of a sense of humor about his dad. He was also bouncing in and out of the news to questions about Jeff, and was driving us nuts. "Do you think he's okay? What do you think made him do that? Think he needs vitamins?" then back to the news. Boy, he was uneasy.

Finally, Max called and ended it. He said they were

going to keep Jeff overnight for observation and he would be back to the Roundup in a half-hour; for us to go ahead down and order dinner, and to get him the biggest, juiciest rib-eye in the place and he'd be here by the time it was on his plate. That settled us down; if Max was being funny, Jeff was probably okay. But, boy, he'd sure looked bad back there on the deck.

Max was right on the button; he sat down about two minutes before dinner came. "Looks like he might be just exhausted," he said. "They're going to do some tests tonight and tomorrow and they say he should be ready to go home after that."

"That mean we're going to be here a day or two?" I asked.

Max nodded. "Looks like it. I can't see leaving Jeff in Havre, Montana. He didn't swim *that* bad. You guys call home first thing tomorrow and let your parents know."

We ate our dinner, which was great, but not as great as it would have been if Jeff had been there. Pigging out at the Roundup is his favorite event of the year. Max said if he got out of the hospital the next day, we'd do a repeat performance that night.

Sunday we mostly farted around, watching basketball on TV and ordering things from room service. We visited Jeff once in the morning and then again after the Sixers-Celtics game. He seemed okay; just really beat. Twice while we were there a nurse came in and took blood. Jeff told the second one that was all they were getting. She was a tough old bag and she squinted at him and said, "Listen up, carrot-top. When I want blood, I take blood." We all agreed that was probably true.

Sunday night Max came into our room and let us know we were going to be there one more day, probably, then head for Spokane Tuesday. He'd contacted the Northern

Montana coach and got us some pool time so we wouldn't lose that day of workout. The trade-off was that Max had to let him give us his recruiting spiel. I can't imagine the scholarship they'd have to come up with for me to stay four winters in Havre, Montana. Maybe tuition and books and half-interest in the John Deere dealership.

On Monday we get a morning workout, then it's over to the Arctic Circle drive-in for burgers and fries and special sauce. It's below zero outside and our wet hair lies on our heads like hard hats. After lunch Max takes us over to a local store called the Mercantile and buys a round of stocking caps. Lion picks one for Jeff; it's orange with a blue ball on top. Jeff will love it.

At the hospital Jeff doesn't look so hot. I mean, he's not looking any better. We talk awhile and Max leaves us in the room for a minute. I walk out to hunt down the bathroom, and though it's a small hospital, I get lost and don't find the can. I end up retracing my steps and bumping into Max talking with a doctor two or three doors down from Jeff's room. They don't see me coming.

". . . little early to be saying this, but I think your boy might be in trouble."

Max says, "How do you mean?"

The doctor doesn't have to look long and hard at Max to know Max doesn't want to be bullshitted. "Well, like I say, it's early to say this, but this looks exactly like one we just lost—a nineteen-year-old girl over at the college."

Max catches sight of me out of the corner of his eye and puts up his hand to stop the conversation. The doctor sees me, smiles and says, "How you doing?"

I'm numb. "Something bad wrong with Jeff?"

Max shakes his head. "He didn't say that. My guess is it's too early to say what's going on, is that right, Doctor?"

The doctor backpedals like a disoriented Olympic cyclist, but it's too late. "It could be a lot of things. I was just saying it reminds me of . . . I didn't mean . . ." He stops and catches himself. He's a young guy, probably hasn't been in the business a long time. He puts his hands on my shoulders. "I spoke way too soon," he says, shaking his head, then looks down. "I had a pretty hard time with the other case, that's all. We all did. I'm sorry. I jumped the gun. You shouldn't have heard me say that."

I turn to walk away and Max grabs my arm. He says, "It's not at all necessarily what you think, Walker. Don't jump to conclusions, and don't say anything to Lion or Nortie. They don't need to hear that. It's way, way premature." I say they won't hear it from me. Then, in a fog, I ask the doctor where the bathroom is, and he points me down the only hall I haven't tried. I go into a stall and sit, wondering how the first thing I could have thought when I heard the doctor's words was that we wouldn't have a relay. Jesus. I sit and try to process what just happened, what it sounded like to me, but I can't. I feel my head shutting down: Closed Until Further Notice. The feeling I have from looking at the doctor's face is that something is really, really wrong. God, what if Jeff is dying?

Somehow I pulled it together and went back to Jeff's room. We visited another half-hour or so and I felt myself pulling way away from Jeff, joking a little sometimes, then finding myself way outside the conversation. When I look back, it seems as if I was insulating myself from the wild places my imagination took me. Then Jeff started to drift off, so we headed back to the Roundup.

I'm a disbeliever by trade. I think if you refuse to believe bad news hard enough, it won't be true, so I tried to will what I had been thinking away, but it kept sneaking up on me. Max took us out to a place called the Ski Bowl a couple hours later, rented us some cross-country skis and we whipped around their trails for a few hours while he went back to the hospital to see if they had any better idea when we'd be able to take Jeff out. We skied in silence, mostly—and hard. Either Lion and Nortie picked something up from me or they sensed something on their own, but it was definitely a Stotan ski trek, staying together, picking up speed with each stride.

When Max came back to get us, he said we'd head out in the morning—that Jeff seemed stronger and it would do him good to get back home.

That night we sat around watching TV and pretending to do a little homework. Nortie found Lion to be the perfect match for him in Gin Rummy; Lion doesn't pay attention either. Several times they went clear through the deck before someone threw down the cards, yelling, "Read 'em and weep" or something of the like. Most of the time I lay on the bed with my Government book open on my stomach, feeling the intermittent rush of unreality wash over me as I saw the doctor's face.

What if Jeff is dying?

Jeff could have walked to the van, he was feeling lots better; but hospitals like to make you think you're sick right up to the instant you set foot off their grounds, so he rode in a wheelchair. I was tremendously relieved at how good he looked and tried to assure myself that I'd known all the time he was really okay; that the doctor had only indulged his own fears.

By 8:00 we were well on our way and I was hoping that leaving Havre would be like leaving a really ugly dream. I forgot I'd qualified, forgot Lion was close. Nothing about swimming was important; it was only important to get Jeff

---

back to someplace familiar so he could be his old self again. I couldn't shake the feeling I'd had right when Lion pulled him out of the water and he was so lost, so helpless. What I didn't know as we started back was that he was headed right back into the hospital when we got to Spokane; that they'd wanted to transport him themselves but he and Max had talked them out of it.

I was unaware of what Jeff probably already feared: that he'd never swim another stroke.

CHAPTER 12

February 17

Boy, the last couple of weeks have been a horror show. Something's really wrong with Jeff. He won't tell us what it is and he asked his parents not to discuss it with anyone, but it's serious. Max knows, but he's not talking, either; says he has to respect Jeff's right to keep it to himself. It's for sure he won't be swimming any more this year; he may not even be back in school, and he's no longer part of the Marine Reserves. Jeff's pretty sick.

We know it, but we don't know how to talk about it. When we got back from Montana, he went straight into the hospital and asked that we didn't come up for a while. Within a week he was out, and he called Lion to come to his place. Lion warned us it was grim, and two days later we all went over and found out he wasn't exaggerating. Jeff's losing his hair and I swear he's lost at least fifteen or twenty pounds. He was lying in bed and refused to talk about anything but how we were doing in the water. When Nortie and I got home after that, Nortie went into his room and locked the door. An hour later I could hear him sobbing in there, but when he finally came out to dinner he had nothing to say; and neither did I.

The next time we went over—this time Elaine went too—he seemed in better spirits, but he didn't look better physically. He kidded around some about premature balding—said it was caused by far too much brilliant thinking—but that was the extent of his acknowledgment that anything was out of the ordinary. I got there early and, before everyone else came, told him we'd been thinking of calling it a season; that maybe we didn't want to finish up without him. He was quiet—just looked at me a few seconds, then off to the side somewhere. God, what must he be thinking? The horrible part, or at least one of the horrible parts, is that I want to be strong so I can help, but I don't feel strong and I don't think he wants my help.

I went back to Max to get some advice, but he didn't have much. He said to trust my instincts. Unfortunately, all my instincts say is I want someone to pay for this.

And life goes on. While we were in Montana, the proverbial poop hit the fan for Mr. Wilson, the student teacher in Government. He was called into the office with Mrs. Stevens and his supervisor from out at Eastern Washington U. and told that taking a student to the Christmas dance must have resulted from a severe interruption in his good judgment, and if he slipped up again, he'd be back out in Cheney before lunch period. I guess Mr. Wilson took it in stride, but Elaine came unglued. She whipped into the office about ninety miles an hour and proceeded to tell Mrs. Stevens and the secretaries and three guys from Building Maintenance just what she thought of people who had no business prying into her life. "He's barely twenty-two years old! I'm eighteen and that means I'm old enough to vote and make the rest of my own decisions! I'll take this to court!"

The Building Maintenance guys cleared out and the secretaries buried their noses in their IBMs and Mrs. Stevens took Elaine right into the inner sanctum without breaking stride. She told Elaine this decision wasn't made about Elaine, that it was made about Mr. Wilson. It simply wasn't acceptable for a student to date a teacher.

"He's not a teacher," Elaine said. "He's a student teacher. A college kid. I can show you ten girls in school right now who are going out with guys older than he is."

Mrs. Stevens let her rant and rave till she got herself down to hurricane force and then she said, "Elaine, I know you don't like this, but it's final. Anyone who student-teaches here is in the role of a teacher; I don't care if they're fourteen years old. School policy does not permit romantic involvement between students and teachers, even if it is 'legal.' Experience tells us it's harmful. Now, if your relationship with Peter Wilson is serious, what you need to do is wait until the end of the term when he's finished. *Then* he'll be a college kid, and you can move in with him, for all I care."

Elaine may be hot stuff, but she's no match for Mrs. Stevens, so she got out. As she was leaving, Mrs. Stevens said, "Elaine, I'm sorry it took us so long to come to this decision. The reason for that was your maturity. It almost seemed okay to us too."

When Elaine told us about it later, I was secretly glad someone squashed their budding little romance, but I feigned outrage. Under normal circumstances, given Lion's natural temperament, we might have had a cause there to rally 'round, but it seemed to die in the shadow of Jeff's situation. Elaine did take it to Max later, just to see what he thought, but he said pretty much the same thing. He didn't actually say he'd forbid it if it were his choice, but he said that a student teacher is practicing to be a teacher and that classroom dynamics just don't allow him to be involved with a student. Sooner or later someone would say Elaine got her A some way other than by doing a great term paper and the teacher's credibility and integrity would automatically come on the line. "It doesn't have anything to do with your ability to handle it emotionally, Elaine," Max said, "it has to do with what works."

And all that helped throw another bugaboo into my plans to clean up my act all the way around as a lover and a friend. On the long trip back from Montana, while I alternated from thinking that everything was okay with Jeff to thinking he had three days to live, one of the conclusions I reached for myself was that you should live every day as if you're on borrowed time, and you should be straight with everyone who's close to you. No one in your life should be in the dark about your intentions. So I was going to by God set the record straight for all concerned very close to the instant I stepped onto Spokane soil: tell Devnee right where things were, and the same with Elaine.

Great plan, but when I related the full story of our weekend to Devnee, she held me and rubbed my back and made me hot chocolate and was so caring and wonderful to me that I fell into the trap of accepting it because it felt so good; and that ended that. Then when I thought more about how hot Elaine was over the school's forbidding her relationship with Mr. Wilson, I realized she was in no mood to hear that one of her best friends wanted her body and soul. So everything is as it was and I'm in a holding pattern in my rise to grace and integrity.

Last night Jeff called us over to his place, and though he

sounded pretty good on the phone, I got the feeling something big was up. He asked us to come alone—bring some pizza or something, but not girlfriends. Nortie and I picked up Elaine, and Lion showed in the Jeepster about a half-hour after we got there, around 5:30, with the pizza. Jeff sat on the couch, dressed for the first time I'd seen since he got back; and Colleen was there beside him, running her fingers absently up and down the inside of his forearm. He wore the orange stocking cap with the blue ball that Lion got him in Montana. He was something like the old Jeff, giving a running commentary on Dan Rather's every word and taking jabs at what he calls the Royalty in the White House. We went along with him and for a while it was like old times. He was still sarcastic and funny, and as an audience, we were his. Even Colleen laughed occasionally, though most of the time she seemed off somewhere, and I guess that was my clue to why we were there.

When we'd finished the pizza, Jeff asked Nortie to shut off the TV, then he said, "Guys, I've got this blood disease; I won't give it the respect of calling it by name. Some people live a long time with it and some people don't; it's hard to predict. What they've done with me so far hasn't worked very well. To tell you the truth, I don't think I'm going to be around long."

Lion said, "Shoot, man. It'll take pretty soon. You're gonna be okay. . . ."

Jeff raised his hand, palm out, and shook his head. "I don't think so," he said. "It feels like nothing's going to work; anyway, that's how I'm playing it."

Tears ran freely down Colleen's cheeks and she clung tighter to Jeff's arm; her nose ran. Nortie jumped up to get her some Kleenex, and for a moment ran around in panicky circles before he figured out where the bathroom was.

144

He came back with a roll of toilet paper and handed it to her, then went back to the ottoman.

"First of all, Walk, you said the other day you guys were thinking of calling it a season." He sighed a long sigh and choked back tears. "Please don't do that. That's the last thing I have any part in, and I want to see it go big. I want to feel like I'm a part of every butt you guys kick at State."

I nodded my head and said, "We'll be there, Jeff."

He looked down at himself and smiled. "Sometimes I can't believe this: watching my body wither away to nothing." He held up his arm and you could see loose skin where his triceps used to bulge. "Look at this." He looked back to us. "There are going to be times, probably soon, when I won't want to see anybody. Sometimes I'm in a lot of pain and sometimes I just feel so shitty I don't want to face anyone. Please remember that you guys are the most important people in my life after Colleen and I love you so much it aches. But if I ask you to stay away, please do it."

Nortic was sitting on the ottoman with his elbows on his knees, dripping tears like a leaky faucet, straight to the floor.

"Knock it off, Wheeler," Jeff said. "You're messing up my mother's rug."

Nortie laughed and shook his head and the tears came faster.

Then Jeff clouded over. "I don't like to put you guys through this," he said. "I was going to be strong—be a Stotan—but I just can't pull it off. I can't put this together." He shook his head and kind of leaned into Colleen. With it right before my eyes, I couldn't believe how frail he looked. You know, What's wrong with this picture?

"When we shipwrecked last year," he said, "I thought I'd had it. I was the only one on the boat who could really

---

145

swim, and we were two miles out in the dead of night and that piece of crap was going down like a rock. I knew I couldn't just swim off and leave those guys, even if it were physically possible.

"So we're up there on the sinking deck, roping everything together that floats. The seas get rougher and rougher, and no one speaks a word. Everyone knows this is it. I'm looking into that black water, thinking, 'I'm eighteen and I'm dead; and I *hate* it.'"

He looked up at Colleen, still holding him tight, and said, "Now I'm *nineteen* and I'm dead; and I hate it. But I got a year."

Looking back, I'm amazed at how fast Jeff went through the denial and rage that's supposed to go with death—either someone else's or your own. But he was right there that night accepting it, and trying to get us to accept it too.

"I won't be like this all the time," he said. "It just seems really important to share some of this with you guys—what it's like and everything." He stood up shakily and kind of stretched. "Now, if it's all right with everyone, I'm tired and I want to spend a little time with my lady here, okay? Get your butts out of here, you have a curfew. We still got the State meet to lose."

We hung in there with him and said, "Right!" but it'll take a few days to get that down—that we have to do it for Jeff, without Jeff. Right now all any of us feels is this awful helplessness.

No one wanted to go home with that, so we headed over to Dolly's for a Coke. Elaine took my coat as extra warmth and rode with Lion, I think in the interest of making sure none of us was alone; though riding with Nortie was like being alone for me. He couldn't talk, just stared out the window.

"Nortie," I said, "Jeff doesn't know that he's dying. It's

just that we tend to expect the worst in hard times, that's all. When he starts feeling better, things will look different."

Nortie shook his head and kept staring out the window. "He knows," he said finally. There was no point in discussing it further.

In Dolly's we picked a booth toward the back and ordered Cokes and fries. Lion propped his back against the wall with his pad on his knees, got out his trusty Rapidograph and started drawing. I remember hoping some magical answer would come out on the paper if he drew long enough.

Finally, Elaine said, "Damn it, Jeff's not a doctor. He can't predict this. He could get better. Some people live a long time with leukemia, or whatever he has. He has no right to give up like that."

I said what I'd said to Nortie in the car, that I just didn't believe it was that hopeless and that Jeff would see it differently when he felt a little better.

Lion nodded, but didn't say anything; he hoped I was right, but wasn't confident at all. Lion knows Jeff better than any of us; there is a part of them that is the same.

Nortie said, "He knows. Jeff knows. If he says it, it's true."

I said, "God damn it, Nortie, this isn't Gin Rummy. Jeff can be wrong."

Nortie shook his head. "He's not. Jeff's gonna die." He looked up. "Listen, you guys, the bad stuff is real. It doesn't do any good to not believe it. Remember when I said I didn't open the letter my brother left me for a long time? You know why? Because I secretly hoped it would say it was all a trick, that he wasn't really dead; that I could meet him down by the old river bridge and we could laugh our butts off at this great trick. But all the note said was 'Sorry.' The bad stuff is real. All of it."

Elaine put her hand on Nortie's arm. "Hey, you guys, let's talk about something else for a while, okay?"

Lion's Rapidograph was flying over the paper; he looked to be in that place where he can see everything—soft eyes, he calls it. He was approaching the Stotanland of artistry. "World's just here," he said, sketching a world that doesn't give a damn. "It doesn't give a damn. We're clinging to this round ball in space by an accident of suction." He flipped the page and shook his head. "Any one of us could be gone in a flash. Doesn't matter whether we've been good guys or bad guys. Right set of circumstances comes up: *zap*. Out of the game. Boy, the next time I hold back from doing something because of what someone might think . . ."

I tried to think back to the last time Lion might have held back because of public opinion. No instance came to mind.

Just then O'Brian and a couple of his flunkies came in the door, looked around and picked a booth up near the front. He looked over at us a couple of times and I remember thinking what a monumental mistake it would be for him to say the wrong thing. There is no justice when guys like O'Brian live and guys like Jeff die.

"Screw it," Lion said. "You're a decent guy. You set up your life, use all your best stuff and what happens? Some stupid little germ comes along and reduces it all to sewer scum." He sketched sewer scum, then laid his pen down for a second. "There's a line in a book called *Vision Quest* by Terry Davis: 'you're born and the hammer cocks.'" He closed his eyes. "What the hell are we gonna do now? I mean, what are we gonna *do?*"

Elaine said, "We need to look at it another way, that's what." I couldn't imagine what "other way" she had in mind. Either Jeff is dying or he isn't, but reality is what it is.

She said, "You know, in some cultures, people view death as just another part of life, part of the cycle of existence. They believe that souls or spirits or whatever are everlasting; that they come back; that everything in life and death has a purpose. Maybe we can't see it, but maybe there's some good to all this."

There was almost a piece of hope in that for me: that just maybe all this wasn't what it appeared to be; that one of our best friends dying wasn't the absolute worst thing ever in the world. But Nortie put it back in perspective, quick. He said, "I don't care how many times Jeff comes back or what he comes back as. If he dies now, he's leaving *us* forever. And that's all I care about."

Nortie was right. All the cosmic, philosophical explanations of life and death don't amount to a medium-sized pile of dog dung when your friend is dying.

Lion continued to sketch, his Rapidograph once again flying over the paper. "Tell you what, sports fans. We got to take care of each other from now on. All of us here, Jeff if we can, Colleen, Max if he ever needs it. Anyone messes with one of us, he gets us all. Life doesn't care, guys. It's just there. The only way we have of getting a leg up on the world is to stick together, no matter what."

It reminded me of what Max had said after he stopped to play with his daughter that night in Montana, and it seems more and more correct as time goes on: the set stays the same; only the players go through changes.

I said, "Well, Jeff says we swim. So we swim."

Elaine glanced up toward the door and gave a little wave, then started picking up her things. "Gotta go, you guys," she said. I looked up and glimpsed part of a head disappearing near the edge of the window. It took me a second to place it as Mr. Wilson's head. Old Elaine and Wilson were going underground. My heart sank, but I gave her a knowing look and said, "See you. Be careful."

"I always am," she said, and was gone.

CHAPTER 13

February 24

I don't understand why things won't quiet down. Every time I think the lunatic who designed this year has run out of tricks, something comes up that adds new meaning to "craziness."

After Jeff made it clear that all we can do for him is be there if he needs us and swim like unlimited hydroplanes at State, we got *heavily* into swimming. All Max did this last week was correct our strokes and call out times during workouts. No pushing, no telling us when to put the pressure on. The pressure is on. We didn't even taper off for our meet in the Tri-Cities this weekend, and we blew everyone out of the water. Of course, we lost the meet, but hit personal bests all the way around.

I started lifting weights again. It's not supposed to be a good idea to do weight training during the regular season—you're supposed to take care of that in the pre-season—but when we left Dolly's that night and I felt so crazy about Jeff and so hurt about Elaine and Mr. Wilson and so full of hate for Marty O'Brian and every other unconscious butt-wipe like him, I dropped Nortie off at home and drove over to the Nautilus Fitness Center, where we worked out during Christmas vacation when the pool was empty. They're open all night to accommodate the people who work swing and graveyard shifts at Kaiser Aluminum and some of the high-tech places coming into the area. I must have stayed two hours; set the weights low and pumped out a million repetitions of each machine. I have no idea whether it was good for me or not, but my body is the only place I have control right now, and with the way things have been the last few months, I just want to keep it big and strong and alive. I have to admit I was a little sore in the water on Monday, but it went away as I warmed up, and none of my repeats was any slower.

But the big story in this newscast is about Nortie, who is swimming with a cracked rib, I think, and not letting it slow him down a millisecond. I'll bet that little bugger will be glad when the time in his life comes that people quit beating on him.

Tuesday night after practice he told me he wouldn't be home for dinner because he and Milika were going out for some pizza and a little time together. Milika has been really good for Nortie lately, because she's tough enough not to let him get so down about Jeff that he can't get back up. She's probably the one person anywhere who makes him feel good about himself. Anyway, they decided to go over to the Savage House on Monroe, which is a hangout for a lot of Frost kids, then maybe take in a movie. But somewhere in there Marty O'Brian came along and altered their plans.

It's hard to know what motivates O'Brian sometimes. I

mean, he has to know that any time he starts in on Nortie, he's going to get the rest of us eventually, and you'd think he'd figure out it isn't worth it. But when Marty gets with his buddies and starts showing off, he can't seem to project very far into the future. Anyway, O'Brian comes in with John Dolan and a couple of other baseballers who have been with him over at the community-college fieldhouse getting in some pre-season workouts. They're still in uniform, slapping their mitts against their legs and being cool; being jocks. They pick a table close to Nortie and Milika, and Nortie thinks about moving, because he's tired of O'Brian giving him a hard time, but Milika tells him to just sit and ignore them. O'Brian doesn't even see them, but when Milika gets up to go to the bathroom, she catches his eye and when she's just out of earshot—and Nortie isn't—O'Brian says to Dolan, "How'd you like to have a little dark meat, Johnny?" and Johnny says, "Would I? Would I?" and they get a big laugh. Nortie ignores them—in fact, he turns his back and pretends not to hear. But O'Brian's such a jerk, he can't let it alone. So he calls over, "What's it like, Wheeler, jumping in the sack with a little tarbaby? Pretty hot stuff?" Then, in an instant, O'Brian's *mean.* "What's the matter, Wheeler? You too much of a puss to get a white woman?"

Nortie turns around and looks O'Brian straight in the eye and says, "Come on, Marty. Leave me alone. I'm not doing anything to you. Why do you always have to be such a jerk?"

"'Cause guys like you make the rest of us look bad. A million chicks out there and you pick a nigger. I gotta tell you, Wheeler, I hate that crap."

Nortie said, "I know you do, Marty. But it's none of your business, so just leave me alone."

153

"Long as you're hanging out with niggers I'm gonna be on you like white on rice."

Dolan is still hanging in there with O'Brian, but the other two guys are hedging a little. One of them says, "Come on, Marty, leave him alone. He's not hurting us."

But Marty's on a roll and he doesn't want any members of his entourage jumping ship on him. "Up yours, Masterson," he says. "You don't like it, hit the road. I hate nigger-lovers."

So Masterson gets up and splits, leaving Dolan and the other guy, an infielder named Dave Seigler, to torment Nortie. Milika comes back from the can then and O'Brian backs off a little; there's nothing in the world that would stop her from going right for O'Brian's eyeballs if the occasion called for it.

Nortie is hot. He's sick and tired of getting pushed around, but he's determined to make this a nice night with Milika and he knows if he says anything, she'll go right after O'Brian, verbally or physically; Milika's a fighter. So Nortie's quiet, and they dig into their pizza. But Marty has to take one last shot, and as the three of them get up to leave, he puts his head close to Nortie's ear and says, "Hey, Wheeler, I hear your redheaded bodyguard ain't feelin' so hot. Too bad." And Nortie is out of his chair and onto O'Brian in a flash. He's screaming and swinging and diving at Marty's legs. O'Brian shoves his face into the floor and kicks him hard in the ribs before Milika fires a glass at him. The glass crashes against the wall next to O'Brian's head, and by the time the shards hit the ground she has a pitcher half full of beer from the table next to them, and people dive for cover. The cook in the kitchen and the guy manning the bar are young guys, small and not about to get into the middle of this for minimum wage, so one of them calls the cops. Marty sees him on the phone and drags Nortie out the side door by his hair. Milika is trying to get a good shot at him when Dolan grabs her from behind and the beer goes everywhere.

By the time they even hear any sirens, Nortie is lying in the parking lot clutching his ribs, spitting out pieces of three side teeth, his T-shirt covered with blood from his nose and mouth. Milika drives the car over beside him and, with Nortie's help, loads him up. She starts to head for the emergency room at Sacred Heart, but Nortie convinces her to bring him home.

I was sitting in the living room finishing off some math and watching some worthless program on TV when they came in the door. Nortie's face was swelling up and he looked *really* bad—bad enough that I thought maybe he'd been to see his dad. My coat was on by the time they finished their story. I let Nortie talk me out of taking him to the hospital, as long as he agreed that if everything wasn't okay in the morning, he'd go without any trouble. He lay on the couch, kind of laughing, while Milika cleaned him up. The monologue she was running made me think O'Brian would be lucky if I found him before she did.

"O'Brian's a wus," Nortie said. "My dad can beat me up twice this good, and he's an old man."

I remember thinking Nortie ought to have his likeness printed on a bunch of those Joe Palooka punching bags that you knock over and they stand right back up. He could make big money out of the fact that everyone seems to want to take a shot at him.

I got in my car and went looking—first to O'Brian's house, but he wasn't there. I left a message with his mother: "O'Brian, your ass is in a sling," then checked all the places I thought he might be hanging out. I made a deal with Max a long time ago that I wouldn't ever "go out looking" to use the karate skills I've learned from him, but that's exactly what I did. If I'd found Marty that night, I'd have shoved his nose up through his brain. I really believe if I'd found him, he'd be dead.

But he isn't dead. After I realized I probably wouldn't run into him, and had cooled off enough to let it ride till morning, I drove over to Lion's and filled him in. As I expected, he flew into a rage. Lion's loyalties to his friends are as fierce as his aversion to socks, times ten; and he is a man who gets even. But he was able to control his rage enough to come up with a stroke of genius: go to the one person on this planet, or at least in this hemisphere, who *best* knows how to GET EVEN IN A BIG WAY. Terminally ill or not, that would be one Jeffrey Hawkins.

O'Brian had the surprising good sense to stay out of school the next day, so nothing escalated. Max bound Nortie's ribs with a piece of an old wetsuit, and either it worked or Nortie has become such a Stotan he just swallows up pain. When we told Max what happened, I was surprised at the intensity of his reaction, given that he initially takes any piece of news like it's the stock-market report. He got every detail from Nortie, some of them twice; and when he finally stopped asking questions, he looked dangerous.

When workout was over, Lion went to the pay phone at the side of the school and called Jeff to see if we could come up for a few minutes—something really important. Jeff said come ahead.

He looked about like we'd left him last night, only he was in bed. One look at Nortie gave him new energy, and Nortie's story brought back, for a few minutes anyway, the old Jeff: sitting attentively, fingers across his lips, thinking several moves ahead.

"You'd have been proud, though, Jeff," Nortie said, finishing up his story. "I think I got a couple of good shots in before he wasted me."

Jeff told Lion and me to get Lion's Jeepster, which Lion had dropped off at his place on the way over. "Is the winch on it?" he asked.

Lion said it was.

"Good." He got up and started dressing.

I said, "Hey, man, you aren't going anywhere. You're in no shape to be leaving your place."

Jeff sucked his tooth. "In the shape I'm in, I can go anywhere I want," he said, and blew me back.

Good point. Well punctuated.

Lion and I whipped over to Lion's and traded my car for the Jeepster and were back in a little under twenty minutes to find Nortie in the driveway with the mattress off Jeff's bed and a long rope; Jeff sat on the steps. He told us to rope the mattress to the back of the Jeepster.

One of the things you avoid with Jeff when he's working on a project is asking him what the hell he's doing. The guy is Alfred Hitchcock when it comes to creating suspense, and he *never* shows his hand. It was absolutely wonderful to have that part of him back. "This is a full-dress operation," he said to Lion when the mattress was secured to the rear bumper and tailgate. "Stop back by your place and get your duds."

Lion left the engine running outside the Fireside, shot up the stairs and was back in nothing flat, clad in cloth helmet, goggles, fur coat and scarf.

"To the community college," Jeff said, and off we flew, me in the co-pilot's seat, Nortie and Jeff manning the tail gunner's spot.

The Frost baseballers were in the college's fieldhouse, just like the night before, going through pre-season condi-

tioning. Most of them had to drive over because no prepa-
rations were made to transport them in a school bus, so
their cars were in the lot behind the fieldhouse—next to the
river.

We flew in low to survey the target area—Lion's scarf
flapping straight back in the breeze, Jeff in back with both
hands on the plastic machine gun, Nortie just sitting there
with his swollen face, wondering what was the punchline—
and took a couple of passes around the lot, looking things
over. O'Brian's car was right next to the end of the fieldhouse, parked maybe three feet from the riverbank. The
parking lot is new and they haven't put in a guard rail, so
only thin air stood between any of the cars and the edge of
the riverbank. On Jeff's command, Lion locked O'Brian's
five-week-old Mustang in his sights, backed the mattress up
flush against its trunk and powered that sweet set of wheels
right into the Little Spokane River. Then he did the same
with Dolan's, which is a clunky old Toyota. The bank's slope
is shallow enough that neither car turned over, just coasted
down into the river and started sinking slowly in the mud.

We took two more quick turns around the parking lot—
victory laps, if you will—tipped our wings in salute and
sped out.

But we didn't go home. Twenty or thirty minutes later,
as the baseballers came out of the fieldhouse to head home,
we flew back into the parking lot, took a couple more fast
turns and brought her to a perfect three-point landing right
in front of where O'Brian's car went in.

And we sat there.

Marty came out of the fieldhouse whapping his glove
against his leg and laughing with one of his buddies. I
hoped he was telling him about kicking Nortie's butt; I like
nice, tight justice. It took him several seconds to figure out
what happened; and, in fact, we had to help.

"Where the hell did I leave my car?" he said to his buddy, then looked up to see us.

"Is that it?" Lion asked, pointing to the river; and O'Brian went nuts.

"My car's in the river!" he screamed. "My goddam car's in the river! Somebody help me get it out. Oh, God, my car's in the river!"

Nortie said, "Hi, Marty, how you doing?"

It actually took that long for Marty to realize how his car got in the river; I wouldn't want to have his chances for a scholarship. At that point Dolan discovered his was also in the drink, and the chaos doubled.

Marty screamed, "You bastard, Serbousek! *You* did this! You're gonna hear from the cops!"

"Wasn't me," Lion said. "I was home eating when it happened, whenever that was. Where were you guys?"

I said, "We were home eating too."

"Yeah, well, what the hell's that mattress doing tied to the back of your Jeep? I got witnesses to that. Right, guys?"

Several baseballers affirmed that they were witnesses to the fact that there was indeed a mattress tied to the back of Lion's Jeepster.

"This is a camper," Lion said. "I use that mattress all the time traveling around the country. Sometimes I even use it at drive-in movies, but that's another story."

O'Brian started to say something else, but Jeff interrupted him. Very quietly he said, "Marty, your car's sinking. Do you want us to help you get it out before it disappears, or do you want to stand there and yell at us?"

That was when O'Brian noticed Lion's winch. He started to call Jeff a name, but caught himself in midword and let it go. Everybody knows that Marty O'Brian's favorite thing in the world is his Mustang. He must have had to deliver a lot of Aryan papers to pay for that thing. "Yeah, help me get it out. Maybe you guys didn't do it. Yeah, help me."

"How much money you got?" Jeff said.

Marty's eyes closed and his head shot back. "Oh, I get it," he said. "You're gonna charge me. That's extortion. Screw you, I'll call a tow truck."

"At the rate it's going down," Jeff said, "it may be hard to find."

Marty looked into the water. His car was sinking.

"How much money you got?" Jeff asked.

"Five bucks, on me," O'Brian said.

"Empty your workout bag."

Marty emptied it and his wallet fell out. "Lemme see," Jeff said.

Marty took a deep breath and threw him the wallet. There were two twenties and three ones. "Forty-three bucks," Jeff said. "What do you think, Serbousek? Can we help him out for forty-three bucks?"

"It's up to Nortie," Lion said.

"Forty-three bucks was just what I was about to say," Nortie said. "Mr. Redden was wrong, there *are* coincidences in life."

We made the same deal with Dolan for thirteen bucks and came away from twenty minutes' work fifty-six dollars richer.

Jeff sat in the back the whole time, probably freezing to death in the twenty-eight-degree weather, without moving a muscle. When Dolan's car was safely up on the pavement, he said, "You guys better take me home. That's about all the excitement I can take in one day." I wrapped him in my coat and sat in the back with my arms around him, crying where no one could see me. When I first put the coat around his shoulders, I felt how frail and weak he was getting, even through his own coat; and he kind of leaned into me. I thought my heart would break.

We got him home okay, and he told us to leave him outside and get the hell out of there, because his dad would be madder than hell and probably had the cops out looking for him right that minute. "Dad will blame you guys for taking me," he said. "Don't worry about it, I'll bring him around."

It killed me to watch him make his way up the sidewalk like an old person, so unsure of every step; so goddam tired.

So Jeff helped us get even and forced O'Brian to kiss our collective butt in the process. That's what he's good at. It was so good to have him back, even if just for that brief time; and I think it was good for him too.

But that wasn't the end of the swim team's dealings with Marty O'Brian that day. Nortie and I went out late that night—maybe around 10:00—for a pizza at the Savage House, and I swear it seemed like someone was setting this all up as a movie or something, because, lo and behold, there at the big round table in the back sat Marty O'Brian and John Dolan and several others from their entourage. Before long they were glaring and pointing; looked like hard times. I was pretty sure that even with all my self-defense skills we'd be in a world of hurt if they decided to come after us, but I made up my mind then and there that the second it even *looked* hot, I was taking O'Brian *out*.

Nortie and I ordered a pizza and a small pitcher of Coke and sat in a place where we could see them easily. Then I thought about Nortie, hanging in there with me, but surely scared to death of having to go through one more beating. "Listen," I said. "Go call Max. Tell him to come on over and we'll buy him something good to eat. And tell him to hurry."

"What should I say? I don't know what to say to him."

"Tell him O'Brian's here with a mob and I told you to call and get him over here quick. That easy enough?"

"That I can handle," he said, and went to the phone.

I'm not sure what Nortie said to Max, but he was there inside of ten minutes and the flavor of things changed significantly. He sat down, poured himself a little Coke and took a slice of pizza. "Everything okay?" he said, and we said now everything seemed fine. Max took a couple of bites of the pizza and a drink of the Coke and he seemed to consider things; then he got up and walked over to their table. He moved in real close to Marty, his feet spread slightly, completely centered. He squatted down beside him and said, "O'Brian, if Nortie Wheeler has any more trouble with you—any trouble at all—I'm going to hurt you. I'll put you in the hospital."

Marty was caught between those places that have become so familiar to him—fear and embarrassment. "You're a teacher," he said. "Is that a threat? You can't threaten me."

"That is a threat," Max said. "It's a threat I'll carry out. It's a threat I *want* to carry out."

"I have witnesses," O'Brian said. "I'll take this to Mrs. Stevens."

In a flash Max kicked out the legs of Marty's chair. Marty landed on the floor. Max brought him to his feet with two fingers directly on the carotid artery in his neck. O'Brian's eyes bulged. "Hey . . ."

"Don't talk to me," Max said, and led him to the phone by the throat. He reached into his pocket, took out a quarter that he placed in the coin slot and commanded O'Brian to dial. "747-5266," he said, removing his fingers from Marty's throat. Marty turned and tried to run, and Max kicked his legs out so quick I didn't see. Marty landed hard on his shoulder and groaned. Max said, "Get up "

Marty got to his feet and came back to the phone.

Max said, "Dial."

They listened on the receiver together. A voice on the other end said, "Gail Stevens speaking."

Silence. "Tell her," Max said.

Marty stammered something unintelligible, and Max put the mouthpiece to his own mouth. "Mrs. Stevens," he said, "this is Max Il Song. I'm down here at the Savage House with Marty O'Brian and some of his friends. He wants to report that I'm threatening to hurt him if he doesn't stay away from Nortie Wheeler. It's true." Max looked at Marty. "Talk."

Marty started to say something, then stopped.

"Max," said the voice on the phone.

"Yeah?"

"You tell Marty O'Brian to report it to someone who cares. Okay? See you in the morning."

Max hung up the phone.

I have serious doubts that Nortie will ever have trouble with Marty O'Brian again.

CHAPTER 14

March 3

Well, a week until State. Actually, it's not even that. It starts Friday; we had our last double dual meet this weekend, so now all there is to do is taper and give it our best shot. I'm doing all I can to clear everything out of my mind but the meet. There's a print-out circulated every Wednesday with the twenty fastest times in each event statewide, and I'm right up there in the 500 free. In fact, I should be second or third when it comes out this week, and the top four times are within two seconds of each other, so with the right amount of psych, I could be right there at the finish. Nortie's got the fastest time in the state for the 200 individual medley and he's second in the 100 free; he's in the top six in three others, so he'll have a choice of events. Lion's tenth in the 100 'fly and, surprisingly enough, sixth in the 100 free and eighth in the 50 free, which is a race that depends mostly on your start and your turn. I'm alive in the 100 and the 200 free too, so it's possible that we could have an all-around great meet. Too bad we don't have Jeff— we'd have a dynamite 400 free relay. Boy, I'd give anything if Jeff were okay.

All troubles with O'Brian are over. He bitched and moaned all over school the day after the Savage House incident with Max—even took it to the baseball coach—and no one paid any attention to him, except to say he should probably watch his step, that messing with Max Il Song could be a very dangerous thing. In fact, his coach told him if there was *any* more trouble whatsoever from him, he was off the team; that he didn't care what kind of talent O'Brian has—if he can't meet minimal standards of decency, he's gone.

My love life, on the other hand, is not resolved, and the only thing I can do is put it off until after State. I thought I could clear it up once and for all by throwing myself on the mercy of Max's wisdom—go in and spill my guts about Elaine and Devnee and the whole nasty mess, get his advice, follow it and *voilà!* Aquaman is out of the quicksand.

Fat chance. The thing I forgot about Max is that he never gives advice that way. He asks you questions. He asks you a *lot* of questions. Then he makes you give yourself advice. Going to myself for advice about love is like going to Dirty Harry for a quiche recipe. You're not likely to get a good one.

Max smiled and said, "You know, Walker, I'm a pretty good person to come to for jock problems, and maybe even a little light Zen, but I may not be in the top ten when it comes to male-female relationships. You saw the results of my latest efforts at midnight in the middle of Montana."

I told him anyway. He nodded his head several times

while I talked about Devnee and the number of times I've tried to tell her how ambivalent I am about our relationship—that number is approaching double digits—each time with the same result. But his eyebrows rose a few centimeters when I talked about Elaine.

"How do you picture that affecting your friendship?" he asked.

"I picture Elaine ripping my throat out when I tell her how I've been seeing her lately."

Max smiled and nodded. "That could happen. Given recent events with Peter Wilson, I can imagine Elaine might not be in the best possible place to hear it," he said.

"Yeah, you're probably right. But what do I do?"

"What do you *want* to do?"

"I want to forget all this crap and go swim fast."

Max said, "That would be safe. And probably smart. But it might be more easily said than done. Feelings don't come and go on command. Here's a hard one: can you honestly picture you and Elaine as a couple right now?"

I thought about it a second, pictured Elaine in my letter jacket, us holding hands in the hall, smooching in the back of my Duster—all under the watchful eye of my fellow mermen. "Nope," I said.

"That could be your answer." Max's eyes softened. "Walker, I think if there's a time for you and Elaine, it's down the road a piece." He saw the look on my face and said, "Don't worry about Peter Wilson. Elaine will outgrow him before the end of summer. Either that or he'll get invited over to her house and meet her dad."

I laughed and shrugged. "Yeah, well, what about Devnee?"

"What *about* Devnee?"

"No, no, no," I said. "That's *my* question. You are my

faculty advisor. I supply the questions, you supply the answers."

"Is she serious about you?"

"God," I said, "who knows? I've always been afraid to ask her; afraid she'd say yes."

"That could be important information. Maybe she's just having a good time like you and there's nothing to worry about."

I wondered why I wasn't having a good time. "What if she *is* serious?"

Then Max said what I'd come to hear. "I have only one piece of advice about relationships, and I learned it from bitter experience. Be straight. Anything that's unsaid is a lie."

"This is a tough town," I said, looking around his office.

"This *is* a tough town."

So, armed with that and determined to do the right thing, I called Devnee and asked if she'd like to go over to Dolly's for a Coke. I picked her up at 8:00 and she looked stunning, but I fought through that.

"You ever think about what happens after this year?" I asked after the waitress delivered our Cokes and my fries.

"Sometimes," she said. "It's kind of scary, though, because I never know what you want. I've been kind of holding out to see where you get a scholarship. I guess I can go pretty much anywhere I want."

It's true. Devnee has a 3.89 grade average. She could show up on the doorstep of any college in the country the day before registration and they'd take her.

She said, "You know, Walker, you're not the easiest person in the world to read, and I don't like to be pushy, but it would really help me to know what you want out of this."

"You mean you'd go wherever I go?" I asked.

"Within reason."

That answered my question about whether or not she was serious.

That was the point at which I was supposed to say I wasn't sure where I stood in the relationship; that a lot of the feelings I'd had when we started going together had changed; that I needed space, as the jargon goes. First step on the way out.

Anything that's unsaid is a lie.

"Boy, I haven't thought much about it," I lied. "Let me see what happens after State, what kind of offers I get. Then we'll talk about it, okay?"

Devnee said okay and came over to my side of the booth. She kissed me on the cheek and started playing with my leg under the table. *Some* of the old feelings came back up.

That night I lay in bed in my dark room, staring at the ceiling, wondering what kind of jerk I'm going to grow up to be. Devnee's been nothing but straight with me since the first time we went out, and even when I was head over heels in love with her, I always held back some, probably because we're not really a lot alike. I mean, she's always been apart from my life of swimming; I kept her separate somehow from my most intimate friends. Like now I hardly ever discuss Jeff with her because I just don't think she can feel what I feel about him. She knows I'm hurting, and she rubs my back and soothes me, but I don't think she can touch the depth of my fear and my sense of loss. If I thought she could, I would love her. Elaine can; she feels it just like I do. But she's with Mr. Wilson, and for now nothing's going to change that.

As for Devnee, I can't be the cause of her pain right now. I just can't stand to do that. I know in my head that Max is right, that I need to say it all, but I'm just stuck.

We were supposed to be banned from seeing Jeff for at

least a month by his dad, because he was so pissed at us for taking Jeff with us on our bombing mission, but that lasted only a couple of days. Jeff convinced his dad that it was his doing and warned him that he'd be pretty sorry if Jeff croaked without being able to see his friends. He did have a couple of bad days afterward, though, so our visits were cut short. God, I just can't imagine nothingness where Jeff is. What's going to take up his space? We've talked it to death, no pun intended, and nothing about it changes.

Max called us—Elaine included—into his office yesterday before the afternoon workout, I think to help us with some of that. "Remember at the end of Stotan Week, when I talked about what I thought the lessons were?" he asked, and we nodded our heads. "Remember I said when it comes time to meet the Dragon, you'll know the depth of your well? Well, the Dragon is here. Nothing they've done with Jeff seems to have made much difference in his condition, which is deteriorating, slowly but consistently."

A collective sigh went out of us.

"I haven't talked much about this with you for a couple of reasons," he said. "I wanted to let you sit with it awhile, let you see how you really felt, and I had to do the same for myself. Jeff is real important to me; I've known him and his folks for a long time."

Max put his head down and stared at the floor, then looked up at us with clear eyes. "The point is, the Dragon is here and he seems to have come in the form of Death. He's ugly. And, guys, what you learned about yourselves during Stotan Week can help you here. The magic wasn't in gritting your teeth and enduring the pain with no show of emotion. It was in letting go; accepting reality; what *is,* as they say. That's the only way you'll find strength to deal with this. It doesn't mean Jeff can't go into remission or get better or whatever, but so far nothing like that has happened. We all need to accept that Jeff may be gone. I know you've spent the past month asking why, but 'why' isn't the question. All that's important is that it's so."

Max stood up. "I'm here if anyone needs me. More likely than not, you'll need each other." He shook his head. "Guys, I wish I could make it different."

CHAPTER 15

March 10

Well, the 1985 State swimming meet is history. Turns out you couldn't have beat me in the 500 free with a club. It was my race and my time. But in no way was it the highlight of my meet, believe it or not.

Jeff gave us a little false hope a couple days before the meet—he actually seemed to improve some. Maybe it was wishful thinking, but he looked to have more color in his face and he was certainly in better spirits. We even talked among ourselves about figuring out a way he could come along and watch, though it was never really a possibility. The fact that the three of us had the overwhelming feeling we were doing it for him made us want him to come see us do it. But Thursday morning, just before we left, I called his house to let him know he was with us in spirit if not in body, and found out that he'd been admitted to Sacred Heart again the night before. Damn it.

The school held a short convocation for us at the end of first period in the gym. Mrs. Stevens gave a little speech about how proud of us they were, and said she was confident we wouldn't let them down. Max said a few words, which he botched miserably; a public speaker he ain't. I was supposed to say something as team captain, and all I could think of was this: "We thank you all for supporting us and we want you to know that every stroke we swim will be for Jeff Hawkins." It was then I realized why I'd been dreading the meet so much. I really had been, though I never mentioned it—not even to myself. I dreaded it because as soon as it was over, there was nothing else to offer Jeff. Workouts have been fierce since we got back from Montana, mostly because we knew we wanted to place absolutely as high as we could in every event in Jeff's name: so he'd know we were with him; so he'd *feel* it. We wanted to take the thing we do best, do our best in it, then give it to him. After all, that's what he asked for.

But when it's over, what is there?

Outside, in front of the school, as we loaded our suitcases and workout bags into the van, the pep band played the school fight song and the cheerleaders did a couple of silly cheers they converted over from football and basketball to fit swimming. That isn't easy. The sidewalk was icy and two of them fell on their butts before it was over. It felt warm and good to have all the attention, and for the first time this year I actually wanted to bring home something for the school too, instead of just for us. I guess maybe we've been a little arrogant. It isn't the student body that's terminating the swimming program.

Devnee came up as we closed the back of the van and pecked me on the cheek and wished me good luck, and the crowd cheered, calling for a big smooch, but I don't do that stuff in public, so I clowned around and slapped her on the butt and we started loading ourselves into the van. I felt a tug on my coat and turned to see Elaine. She hugged me and said to kick some ass, which I promised I would. Then she said, "Walker, I know what's been going on with you," and I gave her a look of complete uncomprehension.

"You know what I'm talking about," she said, looking through me.

I gave it up and nodded. "Yeah," I said. "I know what you're talking about. Sorry." Then, "How did you know?"

She smiled, closing her eyes, and shook her head. "You think you're *so* cool about things. I'm a witch, Walker. You've always known that. I know everything."

"Well," I said, embarrassed, "it wouldn't have worked."

She nodded and raised her eyebrows and said, "Yeah."

In the van, as we passed Four Lakes and Cheney, Nortie moved into the portable seat, snatched Lion's sketching pad out of his hands, threw down a deck of cards and said, "Deal."

Lion closed his eyes and his chin dropped to his chest, and he dealt what turned out to be one of the sorriest Gin Rummy games in modern history. I tell you, the most useful thing either of those two can do with a playing card is to clothes-pin it to the spokes of his bicycle wheel. Sitting up front, talking to Max and listening to the radio, I could remember which cards had been played better than either of them could.

It was a bright day, a hopeful day. This has been a tough winter, probably more snow and cold weather than any winter since I was born, and there have been very few days when anyone saw the sun, but this day was blue and bright and eastern Washington stretched like a soft cotton blanket as far as we could see in any direction. Horses and cattle in the fields modeled shaggy fur coats and hung close to-gether; smoke from farmhouse chimneys drifted straight up, like maybe we were going to get rid of this cold, mis-erable winter straight out through the ceiling. Max made great time; the roads were bare and dry and he was deter-mined to get us there as fast as possible so we could go over to the pool at the University of Washington, get a good warmup and still have plenty of time for rest. Max coddled us as much on this trip as he worked us in Stotan Week.

The sense of anticipation increased in intensity as we passed by Cle Elum and headed up into the Cascades, over Snowqualmie Pass with its high mountain lakes; then be-came keener as we moved down toward North Bend and Issaquah, and a half-dozen other little towns named after the people who were really here first. The closer we got to Seattle, the more focused I felt—that city means competi-tion to me, running all the way back to my AAU days. We caught I-5 heading north and took the Lake Washington exit to our motel, right on the shore. We checked in, hung our clothes out, then located the sauna and Jacuzzi. Max took us over to the University then and ran us through about 2,000 yards of half-to-three-quarters-effort workout. I knew from the moment we hit the water he'd tapered me just right. I felt I could have jumped into Puget Sound, swum out to the ocean and kept going right on to Japan, or whatever's over there. God, I was strong.

We went out for a good fish dinner, then walked around the Wharf awhile, feeling the calm and enjoying the coastal weather, which seemed almost balmy compared to Spokane all winter. But we were missing a piece; there was no red-headed loon giving us running commentary on the history of every boat and building we passed, no one to bring it alive in that exaggerated, sometimes ludicrous way Jeff has of presenting The Truth.

We went back to the motel early and lay around my room, watching TV and shooting the bull. Max turned in early, around 9:30, but we stayed up for *Hill Street Blues*. I remember thinking I was going to swim my 500 like I imagined Mick Belker would, snarling and growling all the way. I lay awake awhile after everyone had gone to their rooms, staring at the ceiling in the dark, visualizing my race, the way Max taught me. I must have swum through it ten or fifteen times, feeling myself putting on the pressure in those middle laps, swimming my own race, allowing no one to pull me into their pace. I saw the prelims first, qualifying in the top four so I'd have an inside lane in the finals. I knew, because of the way they set up the prelims, that I wouldn't get the best competition there, but that I needed a good time. That was okay; I've said it before, I'm good against the clock. I drifted off to the rhythm of my two-beat kick.

Max had us over at the pool by 8:00 the next morning. The 500 prelims are the first event of the meet and he wanted to give me plenty of time to warm up. The defending champ was a senior from Wilson High School in Tacoma, a full-blooded Indian named Charlie Knows-His-Guns, and I stood up in the stands for a while watching him warm up. What a sweet swimmer he is, long and lean, not a whole lot of muscle definition, but smooth and flowing, with long arms and huge hands—big paddles, Max says. He seemed to shoot into each turn, accelerating off the wall like a rocket. I vowed to see him up close later on, for all the marbles.

It was surprising to see how sort of famous we were. Nortie has been a hot number at State for four years, so swimmers always approach him, but my name is new as a threat, so I hadn't had the celebrity experience before, and I have to say it's all right. Most of the really good swimmers are on the coast, and see us only at State because we spend most of the season on the eastern side of the state and in Idaho and Montana. To them we're just names and times on a print-out, though a few are kids we know from the old days in AAU.

My 500 prelim is a breeze. I qualify second to Charlie and feel like I'm holding back all the way; and the splits are my fastest ever. Nortie qualifies first in the 200 IM and Lion makes the consolation finals in the 100 'fly. We're hot.

After a good rest back at the motel, Max brings me over to the pool an hour before the finals and runs me through a thousand yards or so of pacing.

"Give me a fifty-five-second hundred," he says, and I'm within two tenths. "Another one," and he gets it.

"Give me a fifty-three," he says, and I turn up the heat. The pool fills up with other swimmers and I get into the circle patterns. Some lanes are for continuous swimming, some for 50s, some for 100s; one for sprints. I switch in and out of each at Max's command, giving him back exactly the pacing he asks for. We are *in* tune. I blow it out with eight 25-yard sprints, then get out and dry off; and wait.

The State meet is a big deal over here. *Swimming* is a big deal. The stands start to fill, and ten minutes before the race they're packed. Adrenaline flows like a river through me.

They introduce us one by one, and we stand on the block facing the crowd, like in the Olympics. Charlie Knows-His-Guns is a hero over here and gets a huge ovation. He's gracious, almost elegant, as he shakes my hand and says, "Go for it."

I say, "You too," and the starter calls us to the blocks. At the gun, we're off exactly together; no advantage. I've got the power, Charlie's got the finesse. I pull ahead toward the middle of each lap, he catches me on each turn. Coming off the wall through the first 100, we're neck and neck. I'm swimming easy, really strong, but so is Charlie. Going into the turn at the end of the eighth lap, Charlie pulls ahead a little, maybe a tenth of a body length, and holds it through lap fourteen. On fifteen I pull even, then ahead a little on seventeen. He eats me up on the turn; he's like a slingshot coming off the wall, but I pull even again before the turn going into nineteen. But I somehow get in too close to the wall on the flip—God, I *never* do that—and bring my heel down solid on the edge and lay it open. Pain shoots up my leg and I know I'm trailing blood; but I don't actually lose much because I find the wall quick and get a strong push-off. Charlie gains a hair. My heel is on fire! I hear Max in my head: You can either let it stop you or take it with you.

When I think back, I might have lost the race if I hadn't mangled my foot. It hurt so bad I forgot about my burning lungs and my arms and pecs starting to go. I just hauled it out—touched Charlie Knows-His-Guns out by three hundredths of a second. The first thing I heard when I touched and looked up at the clock to see my new state record was Nortie and Lion up on the deck screaming, "Stotan! Stotan! Stotan!" Then Max was there with a gauze pad and a towel to wrap my foot, and a big, big grin.

I got back from the University Medical Center with the Wilson High School trainer, who volunteered to take me there, in time to see Nortie win the IM by a half-body length, but I missed Lion's eighth-place finish in the 'fly: both personal bests, and Nortie's a state record. The doctor at the Med Center who stitched my heel told me not to swim anymore or I'd wreck his handiwork. I said if I did, I'd be back to give him another shot at it; that I had the 200 tomorrow. He must have been a jock himself, because he said to ask for him.

I did swim, though my foot hurt so bad pushing off the

wall in the 200 that I qualified ninth and had to settle for that place in the consolation finals too. Nortie went on to win the 400 IM and place third in the 100 back, so, for such a small team, we amassed quite a few points.

On the second day, at the break between the prelims and the finals, during the coaches' meeting, I got Max to ask the meet directors and other coaches if they'd let us swim three legs of the 400 free relay, kind of as a tribute to Jeff, and to see where we might have placed. It's a nine-lane pool and there are only six qualifiers, so there was room to do it without bothering anyone. The unanimous decision was that we couldn't, mostly because if it turned out to be any kind of distraction at all, someone could protest the race. Max accepted their decision and delivered it to us.

"You guys willing to go for it?" Lion asked, as soon as Max was out of earshot.

We looked at him.

"For Jeff?" he said.

"How?" Nortie asked.

"Trust me."

As the announcement came over the speaker system for the entries in the 400 freestyle relay, the final race of the State meet, we moved down through the crowd toward the deck, sweatshirt hoods pulled over our heads, clad in Wilson High School warmups appropriated by Lionel Serbousek from several Wilson swimmers who thought it was a *great* idea. Wilson qualified both their A and B teams for the finals, so there were Wilson warmups all over the deck and we blended right in. We went over and sat against the wall, waiting for the introductions to end. When they named the sixth-place qualifier, I started to shed my warmup and the sweats underneath, then sort of sauntered toward the ninth lane and, as the starter called them to their marks, stepped up on the block. He hesitated a second, and I thought the jig was up, but he pulled the trigger and I was off like a shot. Nortie said there was a little confusion then, with a couple of meet officials running around asking questions and jumping into a quick huddle, but the decision was to go.

The pain in my foot didn't exist; I was in and out of my turns fast and hard. I couldn't see the rest of the field, but when you're going a hundred yards, it doesn't matter; there's only one way to do it, and that's as fast as you can. I touched with the leaders and Lion was stretched out over the water as I glanced up—a perfect start. He was all power; held even with the top two teams all the way. Just after his second turn I felt a hand on my shoulder and turned, face to face with the meet director. He said, "We told you not to do this."

"I know," I said. "I'm sorry."

"Sorry may not be good enough. Tell your third man not to go."

I looked him in the eye and said, "Our friend is dying," and he seemed to soften a little, but he said, "This could cost your whole team disqualification."

I glanced up behind him to see Max working his way through the crowd. His stopwatch was in his hand, obviously running. I smiled at the director and said, "Nortie's going to swim."

It didn't really matter what I said to the director, I'd have had to hog-tie Nortie to stop him from swimming. He was already on the block and, as Lion powered in for the touch, shot out over the water.

"I suppose you can take back our medals and points," I said, "but you can't take back the act." I put my hand on his shoulder. "Our friend is dying."

Nortie swam like a man possessed, pulling easily away

from the field. Most teams swim their slowest legs in the second or third position and their fastest man last, so he needed a good lead—and, boy, he got it, looking like some kind of medium-sized nuclear torpedo. He touched, glanced quickly at the clock; you could see his little computer brain figuring what our time would have been had Jeff been there at his best. He smiled, gave a big nod and got out, waiting for the winners.

The lane ropes they use nowadays, for important meets at least, are a series of large round plastic fine-mesh cylinders, designed to keep any wave action from spilling over into the adjacent lane, so while the fury of the fourth leg boiled in the middle six lanes, our lane nine stood smooth as glass, the reflection of the overhead lights shining back at us and the ghost of Jeffrey Hawkins shooting through the still water. We stood there by the block watching it as Max approached from behind and slid his arms around our wet shoulders. "Pretty good swim," he said, and Nortie burst into tears.

Something about the joy and pain of that moment, something about the excruciating contrast, made me feel that no matter what happens now, my life has been worth it. What a ride.

As the last Wilson swimmer approached the touch pad, Nortie came to and his eyes locked in on the clock. When it stopped his computer whirred again for a second, then his eyes lit up. "We could have done it!" he screamed. "It's close, but we might have! We could have done it!" he screamed again, jumping up on the block and facing the crowd. "Awful close! Awful close! We *might* have!"

In a second the Wilson swimmers were there shaking our hands. Charlie Knows-His-Guns pulled Nortie down off the block and said, "I don't know, little man, we were awful damn fast."

Nortie laughed, tears streaming down his face, and said, "We *could* have. Awful close."

Swimmers from the other teams moved toward us now, and the danger of losing our hardware and points obviously passed. There would be no protest. No one there was willing to take anything from us.

So there it is. Wouldn't it be nice to make sense of it, get some idea of what it all means?

The remainder of the year stretches before me like an infinite anticlimax, though I'm sure, as spring opens up and we get out the boat and skis, and as scholarship offers roll in, demanding my immediate attention, I'll feel less empty.

But Jeff is still the same, and we'll have to go on carrying the uncertainty of his status with us. God, sometimes in my most selfish moments I want it to just be over with; want Jeff to go to sleep one night, dreaming of himself and Colleen whole and strong, with a life and everything, and not wake up. But I never wish it really, because I can't even comprehend what it's going to be like when he's gone; how desperately I'll miss him.

I think I expected something more out of my senior year, or at least something really different. I wanted to come out of it with more answers than questions; but for answers I got zip. For questions I have legions.

I think if I ever make it to adulthood, and if I decide to turn back and help someone grow up, either as a parent or a teacher or a coach, I'm going to spend most of my time dispelling myths, clearing up unreal expectations. For instance, we're brought up to think that the good guys are rewarded and the bad guys are punished; but upon close scrutiny, that assumption vanishes into thin air. Nortie certainly never did anything to warrant the horror of his life,

181

and Jeff sure isn't one of the bad guys. Look what he gets to give up.

And who are the bad guys anyway? Are they guys like my brother who are so damaged and weak they prey on people when they're down, or are they guys like O'Brian who are damaged and strong and prey on anybody who gets in their way? And what about guys like Nortie's dad? Is it his fault that ten generations of men before him beat the hell out of their families, and he's too mean and dumb to stop it?

And if a guy like Max Il Song can't pull off a decent relationship with a woman, when his own daughter, who he loves *so* fiercely, is hanging in the balance, then who am I to think I can when my most powerful emotion in my current relationship is ambivalence? That is, next to lust.

All questions; no answers.

But I guess I have learned a few things. I've learned that asking "why" is more often than not a waste of time; that it's much more important just to know what is so. It doesn't matter why Elaine and I can't be lovers, it only matters that we can't. And it doesn't matter why Jeff has to go; he just does.

I think my job in this life is to be an observer. I'm never going to be one of those guys out there on the tip of the arrow of my time, presenting new ideas or inventing ways to get more information on a smaller chip. But I think I'll learn to see pretty well. I think I'll know how things work—understand simple cause and effect—and, with any luck, be able to pass that on. And that's not such a bad thing. I'll be a *Stotan* observer: look for the ways to get from one to the other of those glorious moments when all the emotional stops are pulled, when you're just so goddam glad to be breathing air—like when I was standing at the foot of lane nine at State with Nortie and Lion and Max, having won it all, or at least "awful close." Yeah.

But first things first. Right now I've got to get dressed and go pick up Devnee. Gotta set her straight.